D0090790

THE SISTERS GRIMM

BOOK THREE

THE PROBLEM CHILD

Other books in the Sisters Grimm series:

THE FAIRY-TALE DETECTIVES

THE UNUSUAL SUSPECTS

THE SISTERS GRIMM

BOOK THREE

THE PROBLEM CHILD

MICHAEL BUCKLEY

pictures by Peter Ferguson

Amulet Books
New York

Library of Congress Cataloging-in-Publication data has been applied for.
ISBN 0-8109-4914-8

Designed by Jay Colvin

Published in 2006 by Amulet Books,
an imprint of Harry N. Abrams, Inc.

Printed and bound in U.S.A.
10 9 8 7 6 5 4 3 2 1

115 West 18th Street
New York, NY 10011
www.hnabooks.com

For the kids,
Dominic, Kierra, Kiah, Tulia, Siena, and Dan-Dan

Acknowledgments

What can I say to my editor, Susan Van Metre, other than "Bless you"? You made my dream come true and you whipped that dream into shape for others to share. Everyone at Amulet Books was just wonderful, most notably Andrea Colvin and Jason Wells. I'd also like to thank my wife and literary agent, Alison Fargis of The Stonesong Press, for being my inspiration in words and in life. Thanks to Joseph Deasy, whose support, editing, and brainstorming have been the backbone of these stories. Thanks to my personal cheerleaders, Molly Choi and Maureen Falvey, and to Kevin Houser, Christopher Andreoli, and Sherriene Jones Sontag for their incredible generosity toward me in college. I'd also like to thank the Brothers Grimm, Andrew Lang, Hans Christian Andersen, L. Frank Baum, Rudyard Kipling, and the countless others from whom I have generously borrowed; and of course Daisy, who now, unfortunately, is going to get that bath I've been threatening for some time.

THE SISTERS GRIMM

BOOK THREE

THE PROBLEM CHILD

HE DESCENDED FROM THE CLOUDS LIKE AN ANGEL, *enveloped in a ray of light so brilliant that Sabrina and Daphne had to shield their eyes and look away. When he landed nimbly on the ground and smiled at the group, the light dimmed just enough so that they could see his face. The man he had been just moments before was gone, his flesh replaced by shimmering crystal, his eyes by blazing fires, like two small suns shining down on them all. But when he glanced over at Sabrina, she saw that his transformation hadn't robbed him of his quirky, mischievous grin. He stepped toward her with extended arms, and she stumbled back in fear. His smile quickly turned to a frown.*

"What are you doing?" Sabrina demanded.

"I'm granting myself a wish," he answered. "I wanted to be powerful enough to make the people I love happy. I've been miserable. Happy is better. You can be happy, too. Wish for something, Sabrina. Anything. I can make it happen."

"But look at the cost!" Granny Relda said as she hovered over Mayor Charming's rapidly aging body. His beloved Snow White lay next to him, reaching with bony, arthritic hands to touch his wrinkled face. Everywhere Sabrina looked, Everafters lay struggling against the sudden onrush of old age. Many were in the final throes of death.

"Don't cry for them," the glittery being said to the old woman. "The Everafters have had their day in the sun and it was a long, long day. With their power I can recreate this world as a paradise where 'happily ever after' isn't just for a bunch of bedtime stories come to life. It's time for all our dreams to come true!"

1
FIVE DAYS EARLIER

Sabrina opened her eyes and saw a monster hunched over her. It was nearly fifteen feet tall, with scaly skin, two black leathery wings, and a massive serpentine tail that lashed back and forth. Its feet and hands were enormous, nearly as big as its body, and its head, at the end of a long snake-like neck, was nothing but teeth, thousands of jagged fangs, gnashing in her face. A drop of saliva dripped from the creature's mouth and landed on her forehead. It was as hot as molten lava. "JABBERWOCKY!" the monster roared.

Too afraid to move, Sabrina closed her eyes and did the only thing she could. She prayed. *Please! Please! Please! Let this be a bad dream!*

After a few moments she slowly lifted one eyelid. Unfortunately, the monster was still there.

"Fudge," Sabrina whispered.

"Well, *good morning*!" a boy's voice called from somewhere in the room.

Sabrina knew its owner. "Puck?"

"Did we wake you? So sorry!"

"Could you get this thing off of me?" said Sabrina.

"It's gonna cost you."

"What?"

"I figure if I'm going to have to save your butt every time you get into trouble, I might as well be paid for it. The going rate for this kind of job is seven million dollars," Puck said.

"Where am I going to get seven million dollars? I'm eleven years old!"

"And I want all your desserts for the next six months," Puck added.

The monster roared in Sabrina's face. A long, purple tongue darted out of the beast's mouth and licked her face roughly.

"Fine!" Sabrina cried.

Puck leaped into the air, flipping like an Olympic gymnast, and clung to a dusty light fixture hanging from the ceiling above. Gathering momentum, he swung down feet first into the monster's horrible face. The creature stumbled back and roared. Using the monster's face as a springboard, the nimble boy flipped again and landed on his feet with his hands on his hips. He turned to Sabrina and flashed her a mischievous grin, then pulled her to her feet. "Did you see that landing, Grimm? I want to make sure you get your money's worth."

Sabrina scowled. "How long was I unconscious?" she asked. Her head was still pounding from the smack the beast had given her upon her arrival.

"Long enough for me to get old big-and-ugly here pretty angry," Puck said as the brute recovered and rushed at the children at an impossible speed.

Two enormous pink-streaked wings popped out of Puck's back and fluttered wildly. Before Sabrina knew it, he had snatched the back of her coat and was pulling her into the air, narrowly avoiding the beast's attack. The wall they had just been standing in front of wasn't so lucky. The force of the monster's assault sent it crashing down.

"I've got the big one," Puck said as he set Sabrina back down on the floor. "You take the little one."

Sabrina followed his gaze. In the far corner of the room was a small child wearing a long red cloak that hung to her ankles. She sat on a dirty hospital cot next to the unconscious bodies of two adults, Henry and Veronica Grimm—Sabrina's parents!

How Sabrina had gotten into this particular situation was a long, and almost unbelievable, story. It started a year and a half ago when her mother and father had mysteriously disappeared. The only clue the police had found was a bloodred handprint pressed on the dashboard of their abandoned car. With nothing else to go on and no next-of-kin to step in as guardians, the police were forced to put Sabrina and her six-year-old sister, Daphne, into foster care. That's when things went from bad to worse. The girls were bounced from one foster home to the next, each filled with certifiable lunatics who used Sabrina and Daphne as maids, gardeners, and once, as a couple of amateur roofers. By the time their long-lost grandmother had finally tracked them down, Sabrina didn't think she could ever trust anyone again. Granny Relda didn't make it easy, either. They hadn't been in the old woman's house ten minutes before she started telling incredible stories about the girls being the last living descendents of the Brothers Grimm whose book of fairy tales, she claimed, wasn't a collection of bedtime stories but a history of actual events. Granny Relda also told them that their new hometown, Ferryport Landing, was filled to the brim with characters straight from fairy tales, who now called themselves Everafters and lived side by side with the normal inhabitants of the town, albeit in magical disguises that hid their true identities.

To Sabrina, Granny's stories sounded like the silly ravings of a woman who had forgotten to have her prescriptions filled, but there was a dark side to her story as well. These "Everafters" didn't just live in the town—they were trapped there. Wilhelm, the younger of the Brothers Grimm, had put a spell on the town to prevent the Everafters from leaving and waging war on humans. The spell could only be broken when the last member of the Grimm family died. Sabrina warned her sister that the old woman's stories were nonsense, but when Relda was kidnapped by a two-hundred-foot-tall giant, Sabrina could no longer deny the truth. Luckily, the girls found a way to rescue their grandmother and ever since they had taken on the family responsibility of being fairy-tale detectives, solving the town's most unusual crimes, and going head-to-head with some of its most dangerous residents. As they solved one mystery after another, the girls had started to uncover a disturbing pattern. Every bad guy they had faced was a member of a shadowy group known as the Scarlet Hand, whose mark was a bloodred handprint just like the one the police had found in Sabrina and

Daphne's parents' car! Sabrina knew one day she would come face-to-face with the group's leader and her parents' kidnapper, and now, as she stared at the strange little girl in the red cloak, she was shocked. She had never thought the person behind all her misery would be a child.

Sabrina clenched her hands into fists, ready to fight her parents' captor, only to have a pain shoot through her left arm that nearly knocked her to the floor. It was broken. She shook off the agony and fixed her eyes once more on the child. The little girl was barely as old as Daphne, but her face was the twisted, rage-filled mask of an adult, barely holding back the insanity behind it. Sabrina had seen a man with that expression on the news once. The police had just arrested him for killing five people.

"Get away from my parents," Sabrina demanded as she approached the girl and grabbed her cloak in her good hand.

"This is my mommy and daddy," the little girl shrieked as she jerked away. "I have a baby brother and a kitty-cat, too. When I get my grandma and my puppy, then we can all be a family and play house."

The girl raised her hand. It was covered in what Sabrina hoped was red paint. She turned and pressed it against the wall leaving the all-too-familiar scarlet print. The handprints were everywhere—on the walls, floors, ceilings, windows, even on Sabrina's parents' clothing.

"I don't need a sister," the girl continued. "But you can stay and play with my kitty-cat."

She pointed at the monster, which was batting at Puck with its enormous clawed hands. The fairy boy was leaping out of the way of the beast's every swipe. He couldn't keep it up for long. The little girl's "kitty" was lightning fast. It whipped its tail at Puck, barely missing him and sending a dusty filing cabinet careening across the room. The drawers belched open and hundreds of yellowing documents spilled out.

Sabrina turned back to the little girl.

"Who are you?" she asked, but the child only smiled and reached into her pocket. She removed a small silver ring and slipped it onto her finger. A crimson light engulfed the little girl and Sabrina's sleeping parents.

"Tell my grandma and my puppy that I'm coming and I'll see them soon. Then we can play," the demented child said in a sing-song voice. She raised her tiny hands and suddenly the monster stopped fighting. It turned to the girl and its ferocious face became calm.

"Kitty, we need to find a new playhouse. Burn this one down." The little girl giggled and then the world seemed to stretch, as if someone were pulling on the corner of Sabrina's vision, and, in a blink, the strange child vanished into thin air, taking Sabrina's parents with her.

"No!" Sabrina cried and rushed to the empty bed.

The monster opened its enormous mouth and a burst of flame shot out. The folding blinds on the dingy windows ignited and flames crept up the walls, turning the weathered wallpaper into ash. The beast blasted another wall and then another, sending sparks and cinders in all directions. Within seconds the entire room was on fire.

"Sabrina, duck!" Puck shouted.

Sabrina did as she was told, just as the monster's molten spray shot out inches above her head. It roared in frustration and smacked Puck with its long tail, sending him flailing across the room where he crashed against a wall and tumbled to the floor. His shirt caught on fire and Sabrina rushed to him, patting out the flames before the boy was burned. Puck crawled to his feet once more and stepped between Sabrina and the monster, which stood over them, jaws dripping. The boy snatched up the little wooden sword he kept in his belt and bonked the beast on the snout. "C'mon, ugly. I'm just getting started."

But before Puck could take another swing at the hulking

thing, a terrible groaning sound came from above and a huge section of the ceiling collapsed right on top of the beast. The two children staggered back from the pile of smoldering debris that now stood where the creature had been. Puck grabbed Sabrina and dragged her to safety as what was left of the ceiling rained down around them.

"I think this party is over," he said.

"Wait!" Sabrina shouted. "There could be a clue here to where she took my parents."

"Any clue is kindling now," Puck said pulling her down a hallway. "If you get killed, the old lady will never let me hear the end of it."

They passed by open rooms with doors torn off their hinges. Inside, Sabrina saw hospital beds, rusty metal carts, and more sheets of yellowing paper scattered on the floor. Everywhere was the horrible red handprint.

What is this place? Sabrina wondered.

The children rushed on through the choking, black smoke until they found a door with the word *Exit* over it. When Puck forced it open, a blast of icy wind nearly knocked them both down and blew snow in their faces, blinding them. Puck shielded his eyes with his hands and peered between his fingers.

"We're in the mountains, I think," he shouted

"Can you fly us out of here?" Sabrina said.

"The wind is too strong." Puck helped her out the door, wrapping his arm around her and guiding her through the snowdrifts.

They'd barely taken a dozen steps when the wall of the building exploded behind them, sending brick and mortar flying in every direction. Into the gaping hole stepped the massive, scaly foot of the creature. Its head followed, whipping around on the monster's long neck as its fiery eyes searched for the children. When it spotted them it let out a prehistoric roar that sent snow tumbling from nearby trees.

The children raced away, darting into the woods. The leafless trees provided few hiding places and no protection from the brutal wind, which felt like little razor blades cutting Sabrina's face. Their only choice was to keep running. She and Puck scrambled up some rocks to a clearing at the top of a steep hill. It was a dead end. In front of them was a four-hundred-foot drop to the Hudson Valley below. The whole town of Ferryport Landing was laid out before them. If Sabrina hadn't been sure they were going to die, she would have thought the view was rather nice.

"Puck, I . . ."

The boy turned to her. "I know what you are going to say and I think it's an excellent idea. I'll leave you here and save myself."

"That's not what I was going to say at all!" Sabrina shouted. "I was going to ask you if you had any ideas for getting us out of this."

"Grimm, you usually handle the running and crying part."

Sabrina looked down the steep hill. It was covered in snow. "If only we had a sled," she mumbled.

Puck's eyes lit up. He turned around and got down on his hands and knees.

"What are you doing?" Sabrina asked.

"Climb on my back," Puck insisted. "I've got an idea."

Sabrina was all too familiar with Puck's "ideas." They usually ended in a trip to the emergency room, but with the monster lumbering up the rocky hillside behind them, there were few options.

Sabrina sat on the boy's back with a leg on each side of him.

"OK, what now?"

"Grab my tusk."

"Grab your what?"

Puck turned his head toward her. His face had transformed into that of a walrus. He had two long tusks protruding from his mouth and a mustache of bristly, thick hair. His nose had shrunk into his oily black face and his eyes were large and brown. Sabrina cringed, but reached around with her good arm and grabbed firmly onto one of his tusks.

"Please don't do this," she whimpered. "This is such a bad idea."

"The only bad ideas are the ones never tried," Puck said as his body began to puff up. Layers of blubber inflated under Sabrina. Puck's shirt disappeared, replaced by a super-slippery skin. "Keep your hands and feet inside the ride until we come to a complete stop," he shouted. *"Here we go!"*

Puck leaped forward just as the beast reached the top of the hill. The boy's slick walrus body rocketed down the steep slope toward town. Sabrina held on for dear life.

They zipped between trees and bounced over jutting rocks. Sabrina turned back, confident the monster wouldn't follow them on this desperate flight, only to see it plowing down the hill after them, knocking over trees as if they weren't even there. "JABBERWOCKY!" it screamed.

Puck the walrus raced down the bank of a frozen stream, ramping off a rocky outcropping and soaring into the air. The children fell for what seemed like forever, then hit the ground hard, narrowly missing the spiky branches of an oak tree.

Sabrina turned again to mark the monster's progress. It too used the rocky ramp and sailed into the air. Flapping its wings, it soared higher and higher; then a strong wind knocked it off course and it slammed hard against the mountainside. Moments later, Sabrina lost sight of it completely, though she could still hear it braying in the distance.

"I think we lost it! We're safe!" she cried, just as the ground leveled off. Unfortunately, Puck's slippery body was still zipping along as a four-lane highway of speeding cars appeared in front of them. Unable to stop, Puck skidded into the traffic, spinning several times as he tried to avoid a pickup truck. The startled driver slammed on his breaks. Tires squealed and bumpers crunched. Shrill horns filled the air, but the children still couldn't stop. On the other side of the road was another steep hill. They whipped down it, heading right for a ramshackle old barn. Its doors were wide open, and they slid right in, crashing at last into the far wall of an empty stable.

"Let's do it again!" Puck said, laughing so hard he rolled over on his fat, blubbery side. Giggling, he transformed back into his true form—an annoying eleven-year-old boy.

Sabrina held her sore arm and gazed around at the barn. A few bales of hay sat in the corner and an old plow lay rusting on the ground. Several windows high on the wall were wide open, allowing the snowstorm to blow inside. It was a great place to hide, if they didn't freeze to death in the process.

"Grimm, you look like you fell out of the ugly tree and hit every branch," Puck said when his giggling was finished. Sabrina's head hurt too much for her to come up with a snarky comeback. She was exhausted and her arm felt as if it were ready to fall off. Puck must have sensed how desperate she felt, or maybe he just heard her teeth chattering, because he did something so un-Pucklike, Sabrina couldn't believe it. He got up, sat down behind her, and let his enormous fairy wings sprout from his back. Then he wrapped them around her to keep the bitter cold away. It was the first truly nice thing the so-called Trickster King had ever done for her. Instinctively she wanted to tease him for this rare moment of compassion, but she bit her tongue. Knowing Puck, he'd storm off and she'd die an ice cube.

"What was that thing?" Sabrina asked.

"It's called a Jabberwocky," Puck said. "Two tons of teeth, tail, and terror. From what I've heard, they're impossible to kill. But don't worry, Grimm; it's gone. It had its share of the Trickster King for one day."

"We need to get help," Sabrina said, shivering.

"I'm on it," Puck said. He reached into his pocket, pulled out a small wooden flute, and blew a couple high-pitched notes. Within seconds, a swarm of little lights flooded through the open windows and surrounded the children. They looked like fireflies, but Sabrina knew better. They were Puck's pixie servants—or, as he called them, his minions—and they did whatever Puck asked of them, especially if it was mischief. They buzzed around their boy leader and waited for instructions.

"Go get the old lady," Puck said to them, "and bring me something to start a fire."

The pixies buzzed and darted out through the barn windows. Moments later a wave of them returned carrying tree limbs and dead leaves. These they arranged in a pile in front of the children and then zipped away again. Soon, a second swarm returned carrying a single bottle of root beer, which they gently placed in Puck's hands.

"You have served me well, minions," he said unscrewing the top and tossing it into a corner of the barn. He chugged the whole drink and tossed the bottle aside.

"Ahhhh," he said as he wiped his mouth on his sleeve.

"Was that refreshing? I'd hate for you to be thirsty. Maybe

you would like a sandwich, too," Sabrina snarled. Puck was always thinking of himself.

"Keep your pants on," the boy said. "Something has to be done to keep you from turning into a Grimmsicle."

He unfolded his wings, stood up, and leaned over the pile of timber. His eyes were watering, apparently from all the gassy soda, and suddenly he opened his mouth wide and belched. The burp was deep and guttural and, much to Sabrina's surprise, accompanied by a fireball that shot out of the boy's mouth and ignited the firewood. Sabrina felt the fire's warmth immediately.

"I didn't know you could do that," she said.

"Oh, I'm full of surprises," the boy said proudly as a rumbling sound came from his belly. "Want to see what I can do out the other end?"

The little pixies buzzed and twittered. To Sabrina it sounded as if they were laughing.

"Uh, no thanks," she said, edging closer to the fire.

"Suit yourself," he said and then turned to his small servants. "I need you to go back to the road and wait for the old lady. Come and get me when she arrives."

The little lights blinked on and off, as if to say they understood, and zipped away. When they were gone, Puck wrapped his huge, fairy wings around Sabrina again.

"I'm sorry we couldn't save your parents," he whispered.

Sabrina wanted to cry. She had been so close to rescuing Henry and Veronica and they had slipped through her fingers. How was she supposed to fight the little girl in the red cloak who obviously had magical abilities and controlled a hulking freak with a zillion teeth? Sabrina was just an ordinary eleven-year-old girl. She was powerless. She looked over her shoulder at Puck. He was a fairy—a creature of pure magic. Puck could turn into all kinds of animals, he could fly, he had pixie servants, and now, apparently, even his obnoxious bad habits were useful. The boy was overflowing with power and it gave him a fearlessness Sabrina envied.

"I'd prefer if we kept the heroics to ourselves," he said now, interrupting her thoughts. "The last thing I need is you yapping to everyone in town about me being a hero. I am most definitely not a hero. I'm a villain . . ."

"Of the worst kind," said Sabrina, finishing the boy's sentence. "I know." Puck, a.k.a. the Trickster King, had made it clear on numerous occasions that he was one of the bad guys, but lately it seemed that he was always saving the day.

"And don't you forget it!"

"How could I?" Sabrina said. "You tell me every ten minutes."

Puck didn't respond, and for a long moment the children were silent.

"Still, thanks for saving me," Sabrina said as she felt herself drift off to sleep.

"No problem. I'll just add it to your tab," he replied.

2

When Sabrina woke, she was in a hospital room with a clunky plaster cast on her broken arm. Her little sister, Daphne, sat on the edge of her bed, busily scribbling GET WELL SOON! on the cast with a black marker.

Daphne had been through a lot in the last year and a half; both of them had—the orphanage, the insane foster families, their nasty caseworker, giants, monsters, and mayhem. Through it all, Sabrina had protected her little sister the best she could, growing up fast so that Daphne wouldn't have to. It was worth it to keep the ever-present smile on her little sister's face.

"Hey, monkey," Sabrina said.

Daphne screamed with joy and hugged her sister tightly.

"Are you OK?" Sabrina asked.

"I'm fine," Daphne said, kissing her sister on each cheek.

"And Granny Relda?"

"She's good. She went to get a cup of coffee. She'll be right back."

"Mr. Canis?"

Daphne's eyes welled with tears.

Sabrina hugged her sister to comfort her and to prevent the little girl from seeing the tears rolling down her own cheeks. Mr. Canis, a.k.a. the Big Bad Wolf—and her grandmother's best friend—had been trapped in an explosion that had blown up the girls' elementary school. It was part of a plot by Rumpelstiltskin, in disguise as the school counselor, to break through the barrier that kept the Everafters in Ferryport Landing. He had used the students' anger to turn himself into a human bomb, and Sabrina had been the greatest source of his power.

His plan had failed, thanks to Mr. Canis. And it was when Sabrina realized that her anger might have killed their friend that she used some borrowed magic to wish herself away from the destroyed school and to wherever her parents were. That was how she'd found herself face to face with the Jabberwocky and its mad mistress. And now she knew that Mr. Canis really *was* dead.

She hugged her sister harder. "It's going to be OK," she said.

Daphne quickly took a step back, crossed her arms, and forced a disapproving scowl onto her face.

"You're grounded!" she said.

"What?" Despite her tears, Sabrina had to bite her lip to stop from laughing.

"You heard me. You're grounded."

"What for?"

"Being a jerk," Daphne said. "Mayor Charming gave *us* the Little Match Girl's matches. *We* were supposed to make a wish and step through the portal to save Mom and Dad *together*. But *you* ran off all willy-nilly by yourself without even knowing what you were getting into. You're lucky you weren't killed."

It was obvious that Daphne had rehearsed this lecture many times, but the little girl's sweet face and goofy overalls made it hard for Sabrina to take her seriously.

"This is super-serious stuff," Daphne said, noticing the grin on Sabrina's face. "This isn't funny. I'm really mad. Every time something important is happening you run off on your own and leave me behind. I'm part of this family, too, you know."

"Daphne, I was worried you'd get hurt. You're only seven years old."

Daphne's face grew red with anger. "I'm glad Puck did what he did to you!"

Sabrina's grin faded. "What did Puck do?"

Daphne closed her eyes and bit her lip.

"I just want you to know it wasn't my fault," the little girl continued. "When Granny told him there was no way in the world you could pay him seven million dollars for saving your life . . . well, he got real angry."

"What did he do?"

"Granny says it will come off eventually," Daphne whispered.

Sabrina eyed the black marker in Daphne's hand and a bubble of fear rose in her throat.

"He didn't!" Sabrina cried.

"He did," Daphne mumbled.

Sabrina stumbled out of bed and rushed to a bathroom in the far corner of the room. She stepped inside, flicked on the light, looked into the mirror, and screamed. Puck had drawn a thick mustache above her top lip that reached to the middle of her cheeks and ended in fancy curlicues. On her chin he had drawn a devilish goatee. On her forehead were the awkwardly printed words CAPTAIN DOODIEFACE. She looked like a deranged eleven-year-old pirate.

"He is so dead!" Sabrina turned on the faucet and snatched a washcloth off the rack. Once it was good and lathered with soap, she scrubbed her face until her skin was red and raw. She

CAPTAIN

rinsed the suds off to see her progress and screamed! Puck's graffiti was still there.

"It's *permanent* marker," said Daphne as she stepped sheepishly into the bathroom.

Sabrina continued to scrub in vain. Eventually she gave up and angrily threw the useless washcloth into the sink. Puck had pulled some pretty terrible pranks in the past—Sabrina had woken up with a tarantula in her bed, found a boa constrictor in the shower, and even accidentally brushed her teeth with Crazy Glue—but this was the worst. "Where is that little troll?" she cried as she stomped back into the room.

"If he's smart he's hiding from the terrible wrath of Sabrina Grimm," an elderly voice said from across the room. The girls turned and saw Granny Relda standing in the doorway. She was an old woman in a sky-blue dress and a matching hat with a sunflower appliqué on it. Her face was a web of wrinkles but her green eyes and rosy cheeks made her look much younger. She rushed to Sabrina and wrapped her up in her arms. Daphne joined the hug.

"I saw Mom and Dad," Sabrina said, as Granny held her at arm's length to look her up and down. "They were in some kind of hospital on top of a mountain. There was a little girl in a red cloak and a monster as big as a truck. Puck says it's called a Jabberwocky."

"Creepy!" Daphne cried.

"They looked fine, Granny. Like they had been sleeping the whole time. We tried to rescue them but the little girl had this magic ring and before I knew it they had vanished into thin air. Then the Jabberwocky set everything on fire with its breath. The place looked like they had been living in it for a long time. There were red handprints all over the walls, too. Granny, I think this little girl is the leader of the Scarlet Hand. There might be some clues there but we have to go now before it burns to the ground!"

"Sabrina, you've been in the hospital for three days," Granny Relda said in her light German accent. "The place where you saw your parents is nothing but ash now."

Three days! Sabrina felt a sob rising in her throat.

"I'm so sorry, *liebling*. If you're feeling up to it, the doctor says we can take you home," the old woman continued.

Sabrina nodded, fighting back tears.

Just then a nurse entered the room carrying a bouquet of exotic flowers. "Oh, look, our patient is awake," she said, "in time to receive some flowers. These just arrived."

She set the flowers on a table. Sabrina pulled a little card off the side of the pot and read the inscription. GET WELL SOON, LOVE, UNCLE JAKE.

Granny's face seemed to tighten for a moment but then she smiled. "Must have been sent to the wrong room. Let's go, girls. We have a ride waiting for us downstairs."

• • •

Snow White was beautiful, charming, sweet, funny, and intelligent. The only thing she wasn't was subtle. She couldn't stop staring at Sabrina's mustache and goatee in the rear-view mirror of her car, and, after catching the woman's gaze for the hundredth time, Sabrina finally blurted out that Puck had done it to her. The pretty teacher laughed so hard she snorted. Then she apologized.

"Boys will be boys," she said as she steered her car down the old country roads of Ferryport Landing. "They can be pretty immature when they're young, but they get a little better as they get older."

"Puck is over four thousand years old, Ms. White," Sabrina grumbled. "I think the odds of him getting more mature are pretty slim."

"You're probably right." The woman sighed, sharing a knowing smile with Granny Relda who sat in the front seat beside her. "Billy is nearly five hundred and most of the time he doesn't act a day over seven."

"So, are you two boyfriend and girlfriend?" Daphne cooed. She hung on the back of the front seat to hear all the gossip.

"Daphne!" Ms. White said as her cheeks flushed. "We're just talking."

"Something you two haven't done for a few hundred years," Granny Relda said. "I've heard the good mayor has been sending you flowers every day."

"Relda, you gossip! Who told you that?" Snow White cried.

"Oh, a little bird told me," Granny replied.

Sabrina rolled her eyes. In a town like Ferryport Landing, filled with fairy-tale characters and magical creatures, saying a little bird told her wasn't just an expression. It had probably happened.

"When you two get married, can I be your flower girl?" Daphne begged.

"I'll make you a deal, Daphne. If the mayor and I ever get married, you can be the flower girl, but you might be a very old woman by the time it happens. We're only up to having coffee together. I want to take our relationship slowly, and he's busy with the election," Ms. White said.

"Election?" Sabrina asked.

"The mayoral election," Ms. White explained. "We have one

every four years, though it seems like a bit of a waste of money these days. No one ever runs against Billy."

Soon, Snow White steered her car into the Grimm family's driveway and parked. Everyone got out and said their goodbyes.

"Snow, thank you so much for the ride," Granny Relda said.

"My pleasure, Relda. If you need anything, just give me a ring. Until the school is rebuilt, all I've got to keep me busy is the self-defense class. Which reminds me, will I be seeing my star pupil again this Friday?" Ms. White turned to Daphne.

The little girl bowed to her, the way people do in martial arts films.

"Yes, *sensei,*" she said with a big grin.

"Have you been practicing your warrior face?"

The little girl clenched her hands into claws, squinted her eyes, and contorted her mouth so that she looked like she was very angry, though her overalls with a kitten sewn on the front made it all a little comical.

"Very good," Snow White said. "I was very intimidated." Then she wished Sabrina a speedy recovery before getting back in her car and driving away.

"What was all that *sensei* stuff?" Sabrina asked her little sister.

"Granny thought it was a good idea to keep me busy while you were in the hospital. She signed me up for Ms. White's Bad Apples self-defense class at the community center. I've only gone once but she says I'm a fierce warrior."

"A fierce warrior, huh?" Sabrina laughed. "Was that what all the warrior-face stuff was about?"

"Yes, it's to let an attacker know that you mean business," Daphne explained.

"It looked like it was to let an attacker know you were constipated," Sabrina said.

"What does *constipated* mean?" Daphne asked.

Sabrina leaned over, cupped her hand around her sister's ear, and whispered the definition to her. The little girl stepped back and crinkled up her nose.

"You're gross."

Granny led the girls to the porch and dug in her handbag for her key ring. It had hundreds of keys on it, which she quickly sorted through to find the ones that fit the dozen locks on the front door. When she was finished with the keys, she knocked three times on the door and said, "We're home." The last magical lock slid open and the family hurried inside the house and out of the cold.

Daphne had to help Sabrina out of her coat and boots. With her broken arm in its clunky cast, Sabrina realized there were a few things she wouldn't be able to do on her own. She didn't like the feeling of helplessness. It didn't feel natural for Daphne to be taking care of her.

Still, there was something she could do to help everyone and she couldn't wait to get started. She made a beeline to the enormous bookshelves in the living room, which housed the family's collection of journals, clothbound records of everything every Grimm had experienced since Wilhelm Grimm had arrived in the town more than two hundred years earlier. Sabrina was sure there must be something in them about a little girl and her pet monster, but before she could grab a single volume, her grandmother stepped in her way.

"Uh-uh. No detective work today. You're going straight to bed and getting some rest."

"Rest? I've been asleep for three days," Sabrina complained. "I can rest when Mom and Dad are safe at home."

Granny Relda shook her head. "Upstairs," she said.

Sabrina scowled and stomped up the steps to her room. The old woman and Daphne followed and helped her out of her clothes. The whole experience was humiliating. Sabrina couldn't even put on her own pajamas without help. Climbing into bed was equally difficult, and when her grandmother started laying heavy quilts on her, she knew that getting out again was going to be a real challenge.

"I bet reading one of the journals might make me sleepy," Sabrina said as her grandmother added another blanket to the mountain of down quilts trapping her.

"Are you warm enough?" Granny Relda asked as she tucked the sides of the blankets underneath Sabrina, turning her into a human burrito.

"Yes! You could bake a turkey under here," the girl said, struggling to free herself.

Just then, Elvis peeked around the doorjamb.

"Elvis!" Sabrina called. "Come here, boy! Help me escape!"

The family's two-hundred-pound Great Dane let out a soft whine. Despite his imposing figure and a face that said "I can eat you in one bite," the dog had a sensitive, loving nature. He was incredibly playful and affectionate to the girls, and normally he would have leaped onto the bed and covered Sabrina in happy kisses. There was something wrong.

"What's with him?" Sabrina asked.

"He's pouting," Granny Relda said stiffly.

"Pouting? Why?"

"I'll show you," Daphne said, rushing over to the dog. She tried to pull him into the room by his collar, but Elvis wouldn't budge.

"Young man, get in here and say hello," Granny insisted.

Elvis snorted and reluctantly stepped into the doorway. He was wearing a green vest, white booties, a saggy red Santa hat with furry white trim, and a long white beard attached under his chin. When he was in full view, he dropped his head and whined.

"Don't feel bad, pooch," Sabrina said, sympathetically. "I might be known as Captain Doodieface until I'm in college."

"I think he looks handsome!" Daphne cried, wrapping her arms around the dog's neck. "He's my handsome little Christmas baby."

"He's one miserable baby," Sabrina said, laughing.

"I've been working on that costume for days!" Granny exclaimed.

Elvis dropped his head and whined again.

"OK," Granny surrendered. "Take it off him."

Elvis ran around in circles happily, knocking Daphne to the floor as she tried to remove his vest and hat. He gave her a slobbery lick on the face when she succeeded in removing his white beard. She handed it to Sabrina. "You want this? It'll hide the goatee."

Sabrina frowned and shrank down so that the covers were just beneath her nose. "The fairy boy is *dead*."

"Your sister's bunking with me tonight, so you've got the bed all to yourself," Granny said.

"What about Mom and Dad?"

"Your parents are fine. You said yourself they looked as if they had been sleeping the whole time. For now, I think it's best if we just wait until we get another chance to rescue them. I don't believe chasing after that girl and the Jabberwocky is wise."

Sabrina couldn't believe her ears. Granny Relda, one of the famous Grimm detectives, was turning down a mystery, and one that involved her own flesh and blood.

"But what about that building Puck and I discovered?" Sabrina cried. "There could be something that survived the fire that could tell us where Mom and Dad are."

"You and your sister don't need to be snooping with that thing running around," Granny said. "Promise me you will not go back there, Sabrina."

The girl scowled.

"Promise me, Sabrina," the old woman demanded.

"She promises," Daphne said. "We won't go up there."

Satisfied, Granny led Daphne and Elvis into the hallway. When she reached the doorway, she turned, flipped off the light, and stood in the darkness watching Sabrina.

"I can't lose you, *liebling*," the old woman said quietly. "I've already lost too many."

"Mom and Dad need us," Sabrina said, feeling her anger rise in her throat.

Granny nodded but said nothing and then vanished down the hallway.

Sabrina lay in bed for hours brooding over what had happened. Was her grandmother really going to ignore everything that Sabrina had discovered? She had seen her mother and father. She knew what their kidnapper looked like. She'd been at the location the bad guys had been using for a hideout. How could her grandmother say it was best to wait for another opportunity when they were so close?

She scowled again in the direction of the doorway, where her grandmother had stood so silently, and caught sight of something that she realized might explain her grandmother's behavior. Mr. Canis's bedroom door was directly across from her own. Most nights, she heard the restless old man as he fought the demon that lived inside him. His alter ego, the Big Bad Wolf, was a killing machine, but Granny had believed in him. He had been her companion and best friend, and, despite his horrible past, the one person in Ferryport Landing who she trusted completely. Now he was gone.

Sabrina realized how selfish she was being. Granny Relda was heartbroken and certainly not ready to plunge the family into another dangerous adventure, even if it meant saving Henry and Veronica. Her grandmother needed time to mourn.

Sabrina would have to rescue her parents on her own.

• • •

When she was sure everyone was deeply asleep, Sabrina struggled from her blanket cocoon. It took her nearly half an hour to maneuver herself to freedom but eventually she escaped and headed downstairs.

She crept through the house, doing her best to avoid creaky floorboards. Being in the foster care system for so long had taught her a lot about how to be sneaky. She could creep out of someone's house right under the person's nose.

Once in the living room, she reached over and flipped on a table lamp. Elvis was lying on the couch, a place he knew very well he was not supposed to be. He cocked his head with a guilty look.

"You don't say anything and I won't say anything," Sabrina whispered. The big dog seemed OK with the deal. He plopped his huge noggin back down on a cushion and fell asleep.

On the far wall were the bookshelves that held the family journals, as well as the largest collection of fairy-tale stories and studies Sabrina had ever seen, including such volumes as *The Seven People You Meet in Oz, Cheap Eats in Wonderland,* and a weighty one called *The Paul Bunyan Diet.* The library spilled onto the floor and into the other rooms. Some books held up wobbly tables, others were literally swept under the rug. Sabrina had once found a book inside the toilet tank. Tonight she didn't need to search for what she wanted. She reached over and scooped up as many family journals as her good arm would hold. Crossing into the dining room, she placed them on the table and then went back for the rest. Once she had gathered them all, she flipped on a tiny lamp by the table and sat down to read. *Someone in this family has to know something about the girl in the red cloak and her pet Jabberwocky,* she thought.

She found her first reference to the Jabberwocky in her great-great-great-great-great-grandfather Wilhelm's account of his Altantic crossing with his magical passengers. Wilhelm had brought the Everafters to America to help them escape persecution, and from his earliest entries, Sabrina could see it hadn't been an easy voyage.

July 17th, 1805

I'm contemplating turning back. The voyage is already fraught with disasters. Crossing the Atlantic with a shipful of fairy-tale creatures is a difficult enough task, but situations became unruly today when the Jabberwockies ran amok. I curse myself for putting so much stock in the Queen of Hearts's demands. She insisted the beasts might someday be domesticated. The woman is a fool but she has tremendous support amongst the passengers and crew. Fifteen leagues out the trouble began. The Jabberwockies broke loose from their cages. There were ten and together they killed a dozen human seamen before Lancelot and Robin Hood drove them into the hull of the ship. The Black Knight went down with the Vorpal blade and finished the monsters off. Then the rest of us tossed their bodies overboard. Let the sharks have their foul remains.

What's the Vorpal blade? Sabrina wondered, but Wilhelm

never mentioned it again. Sabrina searched the other journals and found no other references to the Jabberwockies or the blade, except in two entries by her great-great-great-grandfather Spaulding Grimm.

March 9th, 1909

When the Lilliputians came to me with the news, I hoped it was just more of their usual mischief, but they were right—a Jabberwocky is roaming the forest. From what father told me, the monsters had all been killed during the voyage from Europe. Could one of the monsters have attached itself to the bottom of the ship and survived the rest of the trip? The magic mirror has informed me that the beasts hibernate for great periods of time, so it could have hidden in the woods without any of us finding it. It's also possible that someone brought another one over from Wonderland, but who? Like my grandfather, I have turned to the Black Knight. I gave him the Vorpal blade and my prayers.

March 10th, 1909

The Black Knight has betrayed me. Instead of hunt-

ing the Jabberwocky, he used the Vorpal blade in a way I never thought possible. He cut a hole in the magical barrier that surrounds the town! He's escaped into the world of humans. I blame myself for trusting the knight; his history is filled with double dealings. But there were no other volunteers. I found the sword lying nearby and have it again in my possession, though it will do me little good. There's no one brave enough in this town to go after the monster, and no one I trust with the blade. Baba Yaga has offered her help. She claims she can entrap the monster with the same spell she and my grandfather cast on the town. Once the beast is captured, I'll find a way to destroy the blade. If the rest of the Everafters were to find out that it can cut through the barrier, there would be chaos in the streets. Perhaps the Blue Fairy can be of some assistance.

Sabrina closed the journal and looked over at the clock on the wall. She'd been working for nearly three hours and sleep was finally creeping up on her. The only other thing she had discovered was strange but unhelpful—some of the pages in her father's journals had been ripped out, a great many of them in fact, at the end of his writings.

Her eyes fluttered. She wondered if closing them for a moment or two might help.

No sooner had she rested her head on the dining room table and closed her eyes when someone said, "Time to wake up." Sabrina bolted upright in her chair and glanced around the dining room. Sitting at the end of the table was the girl in the red cloak. The Jabberwocky was seated next to her, breathing so heavily Sabrina could feel his breath from across the room. The two intruders were hovering over a filthy tea set laid out on the table. The little girl poured a thick, stringy substance into two cups and set one in front of the monster. Its teeth gnashed and a rope of drool fell out of its mouth.

"Have some tea," the little girl said to Sabrina. She poured a third cup and slid it across the table. Whatever was in it was bubbling and black.

"How did you get in here?" Sabrina asked.

The little girl in red giggled.

Suddenly, Henry and Veronica materialized in the seats next to Sabrina. They looked terrified and worried.

"Sabrina, you have to save us," her father said.

"You're our only hope," her mother cried.

"But I'm just a little girl," Sabrina protested.

Just then the shrill cry of an unhappy infant filled the room.

"You've woken the baby!" the little girl wailed.

The Jabberwocky tossed the table aside, sending the tea set smashing to the floor. The creature leaped forward and wrapped its huge talons around Sabrina's neck.

And then Sabrina woke up. The Jabberwocky, the girl in red, and her mom and dad were gone. She sat silently for a moment struggling to calm her breathing.

She glanced down at the journals in front of her, noticing that her grandfather's journal was flipped open. There was something very small written at the bottom of one of the pages and Sabrina had to strain to read it.

Ferryport Landing Asylum Patient List—1955

The Mad Hatter—diagnosis: schizophrenia

Chicken Little—diagnosis: panic attacks

Hansel—diagnosis: eating disorder (outpatient)

The White Rabbit—diagnosis: OCD (obsessive-compulsive disorder; outpatient)

The Old Woman Who Lived in a Shoe—diagnosis: exhaustion (outpatient)

Ichabod Crane—diagnosis: night terrors (outpatient)

Little Red Riding Hood—diagnosis: psychosis with delusions and hallucinations, homicidal tendencies

Sabrina's heart rose up into her throat when she saw the last name on the list. The little girl in the red cloak who had taken her parents was Little Red Riding Hood! Now that it was right in front of her, she felt stupid. *How could I not figure that out?* But how could she? She'd read the story many times. Little Red Riding Hood was one of the good guys. She wasn't evil. She was a victim. Why would she kidnap Henry and Veronica Grimm?

And then it dawned on her. All the rooms she had seen in the abandoned building she and Puck had been transported to had been hospital rooms. It was the Ferryport Landing Asylum.

She leaped from her chair and hurried through the house, back up the steps, and down the hall to Granny's room. She did her best to open the door without causing it to creak and found her sister sound asleep next to their grandmother. Sabrina rushed to her side and gently shook the little girl awake.

"What's wrong?" Daphne whispered as she rubbed the sleep from the corners of her eyes.

"You were mad at me for not including you when I went to get Mom and Dad, right?" Sabrina said.

Her little sister nodded.

"Then get up. We've got some work to do."

3

ou promised Granny you wouldn't go back to that place!" Daphne said as the girls rushed down the hallway.

"No, *you* promised," Sabrina said.

The little girl stepped in front of her sister and crossed her arms defiantly. "I won't let you go!"

"Daphne, I know who kidnapped our parents," Sabrina said.

Her sister gasped. "Who?"

"Little Red Riding Hood."

"Nuh-uh!" Daphne cried.

"I know it sounds crazy, but it's true. That hospital where I found Mom and Dad was an insane asylum. Little Red Riding Hood was a patient there. I have to go back. There might be clues that survived the fire that will tell us where the little nutcase took our parents." Sabrina stepped around her sister and continued down the hallway.

Daphne chased after her. "We should wait until morning. Maybe we can convince Granny to take us up there herself," the little girl said.

"We don't need to bother her with this. She is sad about Mr. Canis and needs some time before she can help us do anything. Unfortunately, every minute we wait is another minute Red Riding Hood can take Mom and Dad farther away," Sabrina said. "She's already got a three-day head start on us."

"But—"

"Daphne, listen!" Sabrina interrupted. "I'm bringing Mom and Dad home with or without you. Every ounce of misery we've experienced in the last year and a half could have been avoided if Mom and Dad hadn't been kidnapped. We would never have been in foster care: we'd still be living at home, safe and sound. If we can get our family back, then things will go back to the way they were."

"What about the Jabberwocky thing?"

"I'll deal with that if and when I have to," Sabrina said, trying to sound confident. Her sister's doubtful expression told her the words didn't sound as convincing as she'd hoped.

"Then we have to take Puck with us," Daphne declared.

"No way!" Sabrina said. Her anger at the boy felt almost physical, like it might bubble over inside her body and pour out her ears.

"Yes way," Daphne insisted. "If you're going to make me break a promise to Granny then you're going to have to let him come along."

"Then I'll go on my own," Sabrina snapped.

"And I will scream at the top of my lungs and wake Granny before you get a chance to go."

"You wouldn't."

"Try me!"

Sabrina snarled. "Fine!" she said as she marched to the door at the end of the hall. On it was a crude drawing of a crocodile that read INTRUDERS WILL B EATIN. Ignoring the sign, Sabrina turned the doorknob and dragged her sister into the room.

Puck's room was every little boy's fantasy come to life, but it wasn't exactly a room. In fact, the only thing about it that even remotely resembled a bedroom was the door that led to it from the hallway. Where the ceiling should have been was an open night sky filled with thousands of twinkling stars shining down on a lagoon below. A roller coaster rolled along a track above the water, and an ice cream truck sat parked on the shore. There was a boxing ring set up off to the right, where a kangaroo wearing boxing shorts and gloves slumbered peacefully. Sabrina noticed a new addition to the room, a mechanical bull splattered with eggs. Dozens of cracked shells and empty egg cartons lay below it.

Puck was nowhere in sight, and the only sounds were those of chirping birds and what was probably a chipmunk digging in the brush. Sabrina shouted for the boy but there was no reply.

"Should we look for him?" Daphne asked.

Sabrina shook her head. "The last time we barged in here we wound up in a vat of glue and buttermilk," she said. She was still having trouble getting the gunk out of her hair. "Hey ugly, we need to talk!" she shouted.

"Maybe he's busy," Daphne said.

"Busy doing what? Picking his nose?"

Just then a spotlight illuminated a book lying on the beach by the lagoon.

"Puck, what's going on?" Sabrina said, suspiciously. Puck didn't reply.

"I want to see what it is," Daphne said and she marched to the lagoon and snatched the book off the sand. She flipped it open before Sabrina could stop her.

A couple of pages into the book, Daphne put the palm of her hand into her mouth and bit down hard. She always did this when she was excited. Sabrina walked over to see what was so interesting.

She found pages of cute baby animals cut from magazines and books glued inside. There were puppies playing with kittens, little foxes peeking their heads out of bushes, a pony racing along a field with its mother, little bunny rabbits eating lettuce, and precious white-furred baby seals frolicking on a beach. Sabrina thought her heart might melt. "Oh, they're so cute," she said out loud.

"I could just eat them!" Daphne said.

And that was when the rope whipped around their legs, flipped them upside down, and yanked them high into the air.

"Puck!" the girls screamed.

The fairy boy stepped out from behind a row of trees. He was wearing a green camouflage helmet of the kind Sabrina had seen on soldiers in old war movies. He had on his usual filthy green hooded sweatshirt and ratty jeans, but he was covered in medals and ribbons as if he were some kind of eleven-year-old five-star general. Spilling out of the woods behind him came a dozen chattering chimpanzees. Each had on the same helmet as their leader but wore bright-red overalls. They all had very eager faces, and water balloons in their hairy hands.

Puck walked over to a small table where an old record player was sitting. He picked up the needle and set it down on the record. A rousing patriotic song filled the air.

"Our plan has worked, men!" Puck shouted over the music. "I told you our enemy could not resist photographs of cute baby animals!"

"Puck, get us down now!" Sabrina demanded. The blood was racing into her broken arm and making it throb with pain.

"Keep your distance, men. Don't be fooled into believing that our enemies are helpless. These 'girls,' as they call themselves, are a crafty bunch. I've seen inside the thing they call a 'purse.' It is filled with all kinds of toxic sprays and pointy things they wouldn't hesitate to unleash on us."

The chimps looked at him with great respect.

"Now, unfortunately, the laws of war prohibit us from killing these two, but I believe we can have them deliver a message to the rest of their kind."

One of the chimpanzees raced to his side and handed him a fat, sloshy water balloon.

"Puck! Don't you dare!" Sabrina demanded.

"Oh, but I do dare, Captain Doodieface," Puck said, turning to his army. "Men, fire at will!"

The first wave of balloons hit Sabrina in the chest and splattered onto Daphne's face, but instead of drenching them in water, they covered the girls in something that smelled a lot like a combination of mayonnaise and grape jelly.

The chimpanzees tossed balloon after balloon at the girls. Each one exploded on contact, soaking them in the foul-smelling glop. By the time the army ran out of ammunition, the sisters were covered from head to toe.

Puck pulled his wooden sword from his belt and stepped over to his prisoners. He poked Sabrina in the side with his little weapon.

"Now you know what happens to people who do not pay their debts," Puck said.

"One of these days I'm going to get my revenge, fairy boy," Sabrina said. "You won't know when it's coming but it's coming, buster. It'll happen when you least expect it."

"Your threats are boring me, Captain. B-O-R-N-G, boring!"

"I am going to—"

"Puck, we were just thinking of sneaking out and getting into some trouble." Daphne said, interrupting her sister's tirade. "We thought you'd like to come along."

The boy cocked an eyebrow. "What kind of trouble?"

"We want to go back up to the hospital and look for clues about our parents."

"Boring!" Puck shouted as he pretended to yawn.

"This is important!" Sabrina begged.

"Which makes it even more boring," Puck said. "I've got better things to do."

"When we're finished we could go to the overpass and toss eggs at passing cars," Daphne offered.

Puck's eyes lit up. "Cut them down, men."

• • •

After the girls got cleaned up and put on some warm clothing, the trio was off. The little snow-covered town lay sleeping, unaware that a flying boy and two young girls were floating high above. As angry as Sabrina was at Puck, she found herself envying him once again. Puck was a genuine pain in the butt, but he had powers and those powers made him useful. If only she could do something special, too.

"I still can't believe Little Red Riding Hood kidnapped Mom and Dad," Daphne said. "She's the hero of that story."

"Well she jumped off the crazy bridge long ago," Sabrina said. "She and the Jabberwocky nearly killed us."

"Nearly killed *you,*" Puck argued. "I beat the stuffing out of that overgrown lizard."

Sabrina rolled her eyes and then spotted the hospital below.

"There it is," she cried, pointing at the burned-out shell. Part of the roof was still intact and much of the right wing of the hospital was still standing, but otherwise the place was in ruins.

"There's not much left, Grimm," Puck said as he set the girls on the ground. The wind was picking up and the damaged beams swayed under its force.

"I guess we start in the part that's still standing," Sabrina said.

Puck took out his little flute and blew a few notes. Soon, the children were surrounded by thousands of pixies. "Minions, we need some light."

Instantly, the glow around the little beings grew brighter and brighter. The pixies went from looking like fireflies to looking like light bulbs. Soon, the entire top of the mountain was illuminated in their dazzling radiance.

"Nice trick," Sabrina said as she led the group into the ruins. Everywhere they looked they saw burnt papers and furniture. They went from room to room, finding no clues. Every file cabinet was empty or welded shut by the flames. One tiny room, covered in what looked like cushions, was untouched by the fire. A crumpled white coat with dozens of buckles and belts lay on the floor—a straitjacket. It was a creepy reminder of what the building had once been.

"Well, this was an enormous waste of time," Puck grumbled. "Let's get going to the overpass. Those cars aren't going to egg themselves."

"I agree," Daphne said. "I am totally freaked out, anyway."

Sabrina's heart sank. The others were right. Anything that might have pointed toward her parents' location was now ashes. Without a word, she turned and marched back the way they came.

"Slow down," Daphne said. "I'm scared."

"There's nothing in here that's going to get you. Stop being a baby!" Sabrina said over her shoulder.

Suddenly, there was a horrible crashing sound and a short shout from her sister. Sabrina spun around to see what was the matter, only to find a hole where Daphne had been. The burnt boards had collapsed beneath her feet. Sabrina rushed to the hole and stared into the darkness below. "Daphne!"

There was a long silence. Sabrina's voice echoed back at her and then she heard her sister's voice.

"Sabrina?"

"Daphne! Are you okay?"

"Yes. Sabrina?"

"What?"

"I hate you!" the little girl screamed.

Puck grabbed onto the back of Sabrina's coat and together they leaped into the hole. Though she couldn't see his wings, Sabrina knew Puck had released them. The two floated to the floor below, followed by several glowing pixies. Daphne appeared to be safe and sound, though a little bruised. Sabrina reached out to help the little girl up, but her sister looked at the offered hand as if it were a snake and stood up on her own.

"Sabrina Grimm! Of all the stupid ideas you've ever had, this is the stupidest. We could get killed in here!"

Sabrina didn't mean to ignore her sister's anger but now that she could see the room, she was dumbfounded. It wasn't a room like the ones upstairs. It was more of a dungeon, with tall granite walls. In one corner, a pair of enormous chains had been pounded into the rock. Against the opposite wall leaned a large antique mirror. Its reflective surface had been destroyed and fire-blackened shards of glass littered the floor below it. But the oddest of the room's furnishings was the baby crib. It was made from solid oak and had a little blue blanket inside, along with a pacifier and a fluffy white teddy bear.

"What is all this?" Puck asked.

"She said she had a baby brother," Sabrina said. "She's stolen someone's child just like she stole my mom and dad."

Daphne opened the top drawer of a small file cabinet in the

far corner of the room and yanked out a collection of aging folders. "I think I found something."

Sabrina rushed to her side, grabbed the files, and flipped through them. Soon she came upon one marked PATIENT 67—LITTLE RED RIDING HOOD. As she leafed through it, a page fell out. Sabrina picked it up. It was a crayon drawing of a family. There was a father, a mother holding a baby, a grandmother, a small child in a red cloak, a hideous monster that could only be the Jabberwocky, and a ferocious-looking dog.

"This is her medical file," Sabrina said.

"Good. Can we get out of here?" Daphne asked. "I'm totally freaked out and my butt hurts."

Sabrina nodded and turned to Puck. The boy's wings were out and ready to fly them from the frightening room. But just then a man stepped out of the shadows.

"Sabrina?"

Sabrina nearly screamed. She squinted to get a better look at the stranger. He was tall and wore a long overcoat. He was about her father's age, with milky blue eyes, shaggy blond hair, and a nose that had been broken in three places. Around his neck were a dozen necklaces and amulets. Every one of his fingers had a ring on it.

"Girls, I need that file," he said as he stepped toward them.

Puck leaped between the girls and the stranger and pulled his sword from his belt. He waved it in the man's face and bonked him on the nose with its tip.

"Owww!" the man cried.

"I'm going to give you to the count of three to run off or you're going to get a bellyful of steel. One . . ."

The man chuckled. He had a quirky grin that seemed incredibly familiar to Sabrina, but she was far too nervous to place it. They'd met so many lunatics and nutcases since moving to Ferryport Landing, she couldn't be sure this man wasn't on the list.

Puck turned to face Sabrina with an embarrassed expression. "What comes after one?"

"Two." Sabrina groaned.

Puck nodded. "Two!"

"Listen, there's been a big misunderstanding," the man said.

"Three!" Puck shouted and then looked over at Sabrina to make sure he was correct. She nodded at the boy and Puck burst into action, quickly bringing his sword down on the man's hand.

"Oww!" the stranger cried. "Cut it out with the sword, kid!"

Puck's wings flapped furiously and he sprang into the air. He did a cartwheel and landed on his feet behind his opponent. "I am Puck, son of Oberon, otherwise known as the Trickster

King, spiritual leader of hooligans, good-for-nothings, and punks," he cried as he landed a kick on the stranger's rear and pushed him to the ground. Puck leaned over his victim, waving the sword in his face. "Had enough?" he asked.

The strange man reached into a pocket of his coat and Sabrina noticed for the first time how unusual the garment was. It had dozens of pockets sewn into it. The man fumbled in one and removed something silver and shiny. He uttered a few nonsensical words and suddenly everything began to shimmer. Sabrina felt queasy, as if she were seasick, and then something unbelievable happened. The man's shadow began to move of its own accord. It pulled itself off the ground with a loud *slurp!* and walked around erratically as if it were an actual person shaking off a case of the dizzies. When it seemed to have finally gotten its bearings, it stepped between Puck and the stranger and put up its hands in a boxing stance.

The shadow rushed forward to attack but Puck blocked its punches, then threw a few of his own. Unfortunately, Puck's counterattack didn't faze the shadow at all; the boy's fists passed harmlessly through the spirit's body. Startled, Puck fell backward, allowing the shadow to get the upper hand. It leaped into the air, did a backflip over the boy, and landed behind him. A swift kick to the Trickster King's rump followed. The boy yelped, then swooped over to Daphne and Sabrina, yanked them off the ground, and zipped up through the hole and into the room above. The shadow man followed, grabbing onto Sabrina's feet and forcing Puck to crash into a wall. Sabrina and Daphne tumbled roughly to the floor. Puck and the shadow went back to fighting, and unfortunately the shadow's master, the stranger, flew up through the hole, landed in the room, and headed straight for the girls.

"Here he comes. What do we do?" Daphne asked.

Sabrina looked down at the chunks of burnt furniture scattered about. She grabbed a blackened chair leg and flung it at the stranger, hitting him in the ribs.

"Oww!" he cried.

Daphne snatched another charred piece of wood and hurled it in the man's direction. Unfortunately, her aim was way off and she hit Puck instead.

"Hey! What are you doing?" the boy complained.

"We're trying to help," Sabrina said.

"Well, stop trying so hard," Puck shouted. "Your help hurts!"

"This isn't working," Daphne said.

"Don't worry. I'll think of something," Sabrina said.

"You do that. Meanwhile, I'm going to take care of that weirdo," Daphne said.

Before Sabrina could stop her, the little girl raced up to the stranger and stopped a few feet from him.

"OK, calm down," the little girl said to herself. "First you bow to your opponent." She bowed low.

"Daphne, get away from him!"

The little girl ignored her sister's warning. "Move into offensive stance," she said, stepping forward with her left leg and shifting her body so that her torso was turned perpendicular to her opponent. She raised her fists.

The stranger looked slightly amused.

"Present your warrior face," Daphne said, crinkling up her nose and eyes and then screaming *"Arggggghhhh!"*

"Daphne, I'm not trying to hurt you," the stranger said. "If you would just listen for a second, I'm your—"

"Deliver attack!" Daphne yelled, cutting off the man's speech. She cried *"Hiya!"* and then kicked the man in the shin. He groaned in pain and bent down to hold his sore leg.

"Deliver secondary attack," the little girl said. She spun around in a complete circle and caught the man's other leg with a sweeping kick. He fell over as if he had been chopped down with an axe.

The little girl continued kicking the man as he lay on the ground. He curled up in a ball and tried to avoid her vicious feet. "Uh, hello . . . I could use some help," Daphne said to her sister.

Sabrina shook off her surprise and together they took turns kicking the stranger.

The man cried out for help and his shadow immediately stopped fighting with Puck. It rushed to his side and grabbed Daphne and Sabrina in its arms. The girls fought against its grip but it was too strong, and while they struggled, the stranger managed to get to his feet.

"All right, I've had just about all I'm going to take from you kids," the man growled as he reached into his pocket once again. Before he could pull out another weapon, Puck swooped down and snatched the girls away from the shadow by the backs of their coats.

"Well, we've got to run," Puck said as they soared into the night sky. Undeterred, the shadow sailed after them, grabbed at Sabrina with its horrible hands, yanked the medical file from under her arm, and flew away. Sabrina cried out and begged Puck to go back for it, but he refused.

As they flew toward home, Sabrina looked down at the cold, dark forest. It might have been a tear in her eye, or the reflection of the moon, but for a second she could have sworn she'd seen someone racing through the woods below at an incredible speed—someone with a shock of white hair. And then he was gone.

4

Puck and Daphne were already at the dining room table when Sabrina came down for breakfast. They had forks and knives in their hands and were pounding them on the table. "We want to eat! We want to eat!" they chanted. Elvis was barking along with the children's demands.

Sabrina took a seat just as Granny Relda entered the room carrying several plates of food. She set them on the table and glanced at Sabrina.

"*Liebling!* You look like you were up all night," she said.

"Slept like a baby," Sabrina lied. She knew she looked tired. When she had gone into the bathroom to brush her teeth before coming down, she saw that her eyes were bloodshot and there were dark circles underneath them. Her stubborn black-marker mustache and goatee weren't helping her appearance, either.

Granny raised a suspicious eyebrow but said nothing, zipping back into the kitchen for more food. Soon, nearly every inch of table was covered with plates overflowing with flapjacks, toast, scrambled eggs, waffles, sausages, oatmeal, French toast, fruit, and yogurt. Best of all, it was normal food. Granny's odd culinary tastes often included black spaghetti, tofu waffles, daffodil gravy, porcupine stew, and cream of skunk cabbage soup.

"What's all this for?" Sabrina said as she enjoyed the feast's delicious smell.

"We're celebrating your return from the hospital, of course," Granny said as she served the girl a heaping spoonful of scrambled eggs, some sausages, a couple of pancakes, and a few slices of apple. She took Sabrina's fork and knife and cut up the meal so Sabrina could easily eat it with one hand. Then she poured maple syrup over all of it. Sabrina took a bite and was surprised to find that it was actually real maple syrup and not some exotic concoction the woman had discovered in Kathmandu or Timbuktu or one of the other zillion places she had visited.

Daphne impaled a pancake on her fork and flipped it into the air. Elvis caught it and wolfed it down without chewing. Daphne took a pancake for herself and shoved the whole thing into her mouth. Sabrina wondered whether Elvis or her little sister had better table manners. Puck had no manners at all. He scooped up some eggs with his dirty hands and crammed them into his mouth. Granny smacked his hand with a serving spoon when he tried to do the same thing with the oatmeal.

"Well, so much for seconds," Sabrina grumbled.

"I was thinking that maybe after breakfast we could dig through the journals and look for clues about Red Riding Hood and the Jabberwocky," Daphne said with a mouthful of food. She winked at her sister.

Sabrina cringed. She hadn't told Granny that she'd discovered that the girl in the red cloak was Little Red Riding Hood. Daphne had just spilled the beans that the children had been doing research. Luckily, the old woman didn't seem to notice Daphne's slip.

"I have a very important announcement to make," Puck said, wiping his greasy mitts on the front of his green hoodie.

Granny raised her eyes in surprise. "Well, don't keep us waiting."

Sabrina scowled. The old woman was intentionally avoiding talking about finding Henry and Veronica.

"As all of you know, I have been saving your lives a lot lately. It seems every time I turn around you three are a breath away from the grave. Well, it's got to stop! I'm retiring."

"Retiring?" the old woman said.

"Yes, I'm out of the hero business. I'm not one of the good guys. I am a villain—"

"Of the worst kind," the Grimm women said. "We know, we know!"

"I thought all the do-gooding wouldn't be so bad if I could make some money, but I extended credit to people who could not pay," Puck said, scowling at Sabrina. "So from now on I'm going back to being one of the bad guys full-time, which, unfortunately, means that since I'm not saving your lives anymore, you're all as good as dead. But a villain has to draw the line somewhere! Bad guys do not save people from the jaws of doom! Bad guys push people into them."

Granny Relda smiled. "But you're so good at being a hero. Maybe you're supposed to be one and just don't want to admit it."

Puck shook his spoon at her. "Don't even joke about that, old lady. I'm serious. I'm going to have to do an awful lot of bad stuff just to break even."

"Oh, so you did this when you were being a saint," Sabrina said, pointing at the doodles on her face.

"I could have tattooed it, Captain!" Puck said.

Sabrina threw down her fork and rose to her feet. "Come here and let me show you how bad *I* can be!"

Puck leaped up, spun around on his heels, and morphed into a parrot. He leaped onto Daphne's shoulder and shrieked, "Shiver me timbers, it's Captain Doodieface, scourge of the smelly seas!"

"Children!" Granny cried as she stepped in the midst of them.

Just then a series of short honks followed by a long impatient blast came from outside.

"Who's that?" Daphne asked.

"Oh, my, he's early. Children, let's hurry and get our coats on," Granny said.

Puck morphed back into a boy. "Where are we going?"

"To the dedication for the new school. Ms. White invited us," Granny said. "Everyone will be there."

"What new school?" Sabrina said.

Granny ignored her and hurried to the closet for the coats.

"But I'm not done eating," Daphne complained.

"Hurry, *lieblings*," the old woman said.

Daphne grumbled to herself as she got up from the table. She peeked in the old woman's direction and, apparently seeing she was out of view, snatched a handful of pancakes and wrapped them around some link sausages. She dipped them all into the syrup on her plate and shoved them into her pants pocket.

"That's going to smell fantastic later," Sabrina said as Granny returned to the room with the childrens' coats.

"It's better to be smelly than hungry," Daphne said matter-of-factly as she tried to put on her mittens with sticky fingers.

Puck crossed his arms in a huff. "I just want to be clear. If a monster attacks while we're at this dedication I am not going to help out. In fact, I might actually help drive the crowd into a frenzy. Are you sure you want me to go, old lady?"

"We'll take our chances," Granny Relda said.

Elvis trotted into the room. Seeing that everyone was leaving, he began to whine. Daphne rushed to the big dog and hugged him.

"Honey baby sweetheart, we wouldn't leave you," she assured the Great Dane and gave him a big smooch on his lips. Elvis licked the girl's maple syrup–covered face and then went to work stealing the pancakes from her pocket. Daphne squirmed away from the furry breakfast bandit. "Hey, get your own, you traitor."

"Come here, boy," Granny said and the big dog darted to her. The old woman quickly dressed him in his Christmas vest and hat before he could get away. Elvis dropped his head and sighed. "Don't be a baby. It's cold out there.

"And what are we going to do about you?" she said, cupping

her hand under Sabrina's chin and eyeing her face closely. "Honestly, Puck. This time you've gone too far."

"Really?" Puck cried. "That's the nicest thing anyone's said to me in a long time."

Granny took a bright orange toboggan hat, put it on Sabrina's head, and pulled down until it covered the writing on her forehead. Then she wrapped an itchy wool scarf around the girl's face all the way up past her nose. "Perfect!" the old woman declared.

Once everyone was ready, the family stepped outside. A bright yellow taxicab with fuzzy dice hanging from the rearview mirror was parked in the driveway. Sitting in the front seat was an incredibly old man with a long white beard. His head was tilted back and even from the porch the girls could hear his loud, raspy snores.

Granny stepped over to his window and tapped on it several times. When this had no effect, she knocked even harder, but still the man dozed away. Finally, Granny opened the front door and pushed down on the car's horn. The blast shocked the old man and he jumped in his seat.

"Great Jehoshaphat!" he cried.

"Mr. van Winkle, we're ready to go," Granny Relda said.

The tired old man rubbed the sleep out of his eyes and climbed out of the car. He wore a black bomber jacket and gray slacks. He looked like some of the cab drivers Sabrina had ridden with back home in New York City, except for the fact that he had a bristly white beard that hung down to his ankles.

"You didn't say anything about a dog," he grumbled.

"Mr. van Winkle, this is Elvis. He's perfectly tame," Granny Relda insisted, ushering Elvis, Daphne, and Puck into the back of the cab, leaving the front seat for Sabrina.

"Has he got all his shots?" the driver grumbled.

"Have *you*?" Daphne asked, covering Elvis's ears with her hands so he wouldn't hear the driver's comments. "Don't listen to the mean man."

"Fine, bring that mongrel, but if he wrecks my cab you're going to have to pay for the damage," Mr. van Winkle grumbled. Sabrina looked the car over as she walked around to the passenger side. It was a museum of horrible accidents. Scratches, dents, and duct-taped dings covered every inch of the cab. It reminded Sabrina of the kind of car that is slammed into walls to check for safety. When she looked inside, she half-expected to see a crash-test dummy in the passenger seat. There was nothing that Elvis could do to the four-wheeled death trap that the driver and Father Time hadn't done already.

When they were all inside, Elvis's big head popped up over the front seat and he sniffed the air wildly. The little old man had a greasy sack on the dashboard that smelled of hot peppers and mozzarella. Elvis rested his head on the driver's shoulder and eyed the bag hungrily, letting out a whimper.

"Not a chance, fleabag. That's my lunch," Mr. van Winkle said before he turned his attention to Sabrina. Her scarf had slipped down, revealing her mustache and goatee. "I've never had a pirate in my cab before."

Puck laughed so hard he snorted.

Sabrina frowned and covered her face with her hand.

"Where to?" the cabbie asked.

"We're going to the elementary school dedication, by the river," Granny Relda said as she helped Daphne into her seatbelt.

"We'll be there in a flash," Mr. van Winkle said. He put his keys into the ignition and turned the engine on. Then nothing. For some time Sabrina thought the old man was thinking about a good route to the school, or maybe waiting for traffic to pass so he could back out. But when five minutes had elapsed, Sabrina looked over to see what was wrong.

"Uh, Granny? He's asleep again," she said.

Granny leaned forward and eyed the man. "Give him a little poke in the arm."

Sabrina nudged his shoulder but it didn't wake the old man.

"Try the horn," Granny Relda said.

Sabrina pushed down on the car horn and the old man awoke with a start. "For the love of all things good and holy!" he cried.

"We're ready," Sabrina said.

He rubbed his eyes once more and then threw the car into reverse and pumped the gas. They were off.

"So you two are the famous Sabrina and Daphne Grimm, huh?" said the cabbie. "Heard a lot about'cha. Word is you two killed a giant, took down Rumpelstiltskin, and went face to face with a Jabberwocky. Tough kids. Never heard of anyone walking away from one of those things, except maybe that knight. What was his name, again? The one with the Vorpal blade?"

"You've heard of the Vorpal blade?" Sabrina asked, remembering her research from the night before.

"Yep, that's the only thing that can kill a Jabberwocky, from what I hear," the driver said.

"Any idea where we could get one?"

The driver chuckled. "It's not like they sell them at Wal-Mart. No, there was only one Vorpal blade and from what I hear it's lost."

Sabrina frowned.

"So you're an Everafter?" Daphne said.

"Sure, I'm Rip van Winkle," the driver said. "You ever hear of me?"

Daphne squealed. Meeting the man behind the famous Washington Irving story was like meeting a movie star to the seven-year-old girl.

"I read about you in the orphanage library," she said. "You fell asleep for a hundred years and when you woke up everything was different. How did it feel to sleep that long?"

There was no answer and Sabrina glanced over to the driver. He had dozed off for a third time. Even worse, his foot was still pushing down on the accelerator and the cab was picking up speed rapidly. Instinctively, Sabrina grabbed the wheel, though she had no idea how to drive a car.

"Help!" she cried. "He's out cold again!"

Granny reached forward and pushed hard on the horn, and the man nearly jumped out of his seat. "Wowie-kazowie!" he exclaimed, giving the steering wheel a quick turn and sending the cab sailing into a parking lot. He braked just inches away from a dump truck. Everyone sat still and caught their breaths. As they calmed themselves, the dump truck started up and then pulled away. It had been obstructing their view, and when it was gone, they saw a shocking sight.

They were at the old school that had been blown to smithereens by Rumpelstiltskin just days before, but it was completely gone. Every board and brick had been removed and

Pho

in its place was a brand-new building. The roof was complete but for a few shingles, the walls had been painted, and workers wearing bright-orange hard hats hustled from one place to the next, nailing the last details into place.

"It's impossible," Sabrina said as she opened her door and stepped out of the cab. How could they have built a brand-new school in such a short time? She knew the answer the second she spotted one of Mayor Charming's witches hoisting the American flag up a shiny new flagpole. Morgan le Fay was one of the Three, a group of witches that also included Glinda, the Good Witch of the North, and Frau Pfefferkuchenhaus, the witch from the Hansel and Gretel story. They worked for the mayor and made most of his problems disappear overnight.

The whole scene made Sabrina sick to her stomach. Mr. Canis was buried beneath the new school. He had died saving the children of Ferryport Landing and this is how the town repaid him. If Sabrina could have, she would have ripped the new school down with her bare hands rather than have her grandmother see it.

"We should go," Sabrina said as she turned to Granny Relda. She couldn't imagine how painful this must be for her grandmother. "This town is heartless."

"I'll be fine, *liebling*," Granny said.

"Hello, Mrs. Grimm," Morgan le Fay said, sashaying over to the group. She was a beautiful woman and the construction workers ogled her every move. "Isn't it wonderful?"

"Yes, for a cemetery," Sabrina replied.

Morgan's smile disappeared. "Well, I won't keep you. It's cold out here," she said as she handed each of them a button with VOTE FOR CHARMING! printed on it in big purple letters.

Granny thanked the witch and turned back to the cab driver. "I'd appreciate you waiting. We're going to leave Elvis here with you."

"No way, lady!" Mr. van Winkle said as Elvis licked his face. "This thing is a menace on four legs."

"But just imagine the tip you'll get if you stick around," Granny said.

The driver scowled but nodded his head. "Make it quick, will ya?"

Granny Relda led the children into the building, where they found a series of paper signs pointing in the direction of the "Dedication Ceremony." The signs ended at two double doors. Granny pushed them open and they stepped inside the school's new gymnasium.

The sounds of celebration filled Sabrina's ears. Every Everafter she had met since arriving in Ferryport Landing, and a whole bunch she had never seen before, stood around talking. A round little robot man made entirely of copper stood nearby talking to a skinny man made of sticks with an enormous pumpkin for a head. A black panther and a huge gray bear talked politics in a corner. There were also ogres, witches, fairy godmothers, an occasional cyclops, an enormous snail smoking a hookah pipe, and dozens and dozens of handsome princes and beautiful princesses gathered in small clusters. A beautiful cocoa-skinned woman in a green dress smiled and waved at Granny Relda.

"It's nice to see you, Briar Rose," Granny called out to her.

"Who's that?" Daphne asked.

"You know her better as Sleeping Beauty," the old woman said. Daphne opened her mouth, inserted her palm, and bit down.

"For the love of Pete, what are you doing here?" a voice said from behind them. Sabrina spun around and found a very small man in a black suit eyeing them disapprovingly. Mr. Seven, as he was known, was the mayor's assistant, limo driver, and personal whipping boy. He was also one of the seven dwarfs. He looked nervous, sweaty, and exhausted.

"Hello, Mr. Seven. Snow White invited us down to see the new school," Granny Relda said to the little man.

"Well, you've seen it. It's great, isn't it? Now why don't you leave? The boss is going to blow his top if he finds you here. He's in a foul mood today," the little man said, looking around nervously.

"You mean worse that his normal foul mood?" Sabrina said.

Just then a tall broad-shouldered man in a purple suit swaggered into the gym. He was impossibly handsome, with dazzling blue eyes, a strong jaw, and perfectly combed black hair. His face was one big smile, and he shook hands with everyone he encountered. He came over and grabbed Sabrina's good hand without even looking at her. He shook it vigorously then peered at her closely. He yanked the wool scarf from her face and groaned.

"Mr. Seven, what are the Grimms doing here?" Mayor Charming demanded. The little man fumbled for words but had no answer.

Mayor Charming was the hero of about a dozen fairy tales. Also known as Prince Charming, he had saved many a damsel in distress—and married a good number of them, too—but somewhere along the way he had stopped being charming and had turned into a first-class jerk. He was rude and condescending, and for almost two hundred years he had been in a bitter feud with Sabrina's family. He'd vowed to someday buy up the whole town and knock down the Grimm house. Still, there was more to him than just nasty hot air. Sabrina had to admit that the mayor came through in a pinch, once lending a hand to stop a giant from destroying the town and then helping prevent Rumpelstiltskin from breaking through the magical barrier that kept the Everafters trapped in Ferryport Landing, but Sabrina wasn't sure he hadn't done it all out of self-interest.

"Mr. Seven, I asked you a question. Who was the moron who invited the Grimms?" Charming asked angrily.

"I invited them." Charming spun around and saw Snow White enter the gymnasium. At one time the mayor and the teacher were engaged to be married, but Snow White had left the prince at the altar, putting an end to their "happily ever after." Sabrina couldn't blame her. Sure Charming was beautiful to look at, but when he opened his mouth, ugh! Still, it was obvious to anyone that the two were still not over each other.

"When I said *moron* I didn't mean you, of course," Charming stammered.

"I would hope not," Ms. White said.

"But why on earth would you invite them?" the mayor said. "This is a ceremony for the Everafter community only. Almost everyone here hates this family."

"Well, I don't, Billy," Ms. White replied. The mayor's angry face immediately softened.

"Well, uh . . ." Charming stammered. "Of course they're welcome."

He bent over and whispered in Sabrina's ear, "Take your grandmother and sister and find a rock to crawl under until this is over. And go wash your face, child. You look like the captain on the cereal box."

"Well, I suppose it's show time," he said, straightening up and forcing a smile to his face. "Don't want to keep the public waiting."

"Good luck," the beautiful teacher said as she stood on tippytoes and kissed the mayor on the cheek. Charming's face turned bright red and he looked a little dizzy. He mumbled a few incoherent words and then walked away.

"You've got quite a power over him," Mr. Seven said to Snow White, who turned bright red and giggled. "I wish we could have you around twenty-four hours a day."

She grinned. "If you'll excuse me, I'm going to find a spot a little closer to the stage."

Granny winked and Snow White disappeared into the crowd.

Suddenly, two tubby men came through the double doors with Sheriff Hamstead, a Grimm family friend, in tow. The two men wore white shirts, blue jeans, and hard hats, and were carrying a set of blueprints with them. Sabrina recognized them as the sheriff's former deputies, Boarman and Swineheart. The sheriff was doing his best to get their attention. To the casual observer the three looked like normal, if a bit overweight, people, but Sabrina and her family knew their secret identities. Boarman, Swineheart, and Hamstead were really the Three Little Pigs in magical disguise.

"I can't believe you two won't even consider it," Hamstead complained.

"Listen Ernest," Swineheart said, spinning around to face his former boss. "There's a reason why we didn't invite you to be a partner in our construction company. You're obsessed with straw. This new school is made entirely out of wood and brick!"

"I'm just saying that straw has come a long way," Hamstead said. "It has all kinds of practical applications. It's the building material of the future."

"I'd agree if we were building something that was *supposed* to blow away," Boarman said. "A kite, for instance, would be perfect, but we're building a school, and one that sits very close to a river, too. One thunderstorm with twenty-mile-an-hour winds would knock a straw building over just like that."

The two rotund men walked away, leaving Hamstead to chase after them.

Just then, Mayor Charming climbed onto the stage and stood

at the podium. He tapped on the microphone and smiled widely. "Fine citizens of Ferryport Landing. Welcome to a new era in our town's education."

"I don't know why everyone is celebrating," Puck said loudly. "Opening a new school should be cause for a national day of mourning."

The entire audience turned to look at the boy fairy. He grinned broadly and waved. The mayor, on the other hand, bit down on his lip and tried to control his anger before he continued.

"I'd like to thank some of the community organizations that made this event possible. First, let's hear a round of applause for our cosponsors and hosts of today's celebration—Fairy Godmothers Against Drunk Driving."

Several blue-haired ladies in fluffy dresses floated into the air, kept aloft by the little flapping wings on their backs. They all wore T-shirts with FGMADD on them. The crowd applauded as the fairies fluttered around the room.

"I also want to thank the League of Wiccan Voters, the National Association for the Advancement of Handsome Princes, Big Brothers and Ugly Stepsisters of America, and Everafters for the Ethical Treatment of Talking Animals. Their hard work and dedication to this important project has been vital to its success."

The crowd applauded again.

"When Ferryport Landing Elementary was destroyed four days ago, I came out to this site and do you know what I heard?"

There was a brief silence and then a loud, squeaky fart. Sabrina turned and saw Puck fall over with laughter. For once, one of his childish pranks was well timed. *Ruin Charming's stupid little event!* Sabrina secretly cheered. *I'm starting to enjoy evil Puck!*

"I heard the future calling," Charming said angrily. He regained his composure and started again. "And I saw an opportunity for our children. When I talk about our children I don't mean the children of everyone in this town. I'm talking about Everafter children. For far too long there has been no room for them at the head of the class. This new school represents an end to that."

The crowd roared with approval.

"I have personally overseen this project, supervising the work, even rolling up my sleeves and picking up a shovel to help out," Charming said, causing some in the audience to laugh good-naturedly. "Boarman and Swineheart Construction have done an amazing job."

"It's Swineheart and Boarman Construction," Swineheart shouted.

"No, it's not. It's Boarman and Swineheart Construction," his partner argued.

Charming cleared his throat and the bickering ended.

"And we couldn't have done any of this without the generous donations of our town's three wealthiest families. Everyone give a round of applause to Little Miss Muffet and the spider—I mean, Mr. and Mrs. Harry Arachnid—Beauty and the Beast, and of course, the Frog Prince and his lovely princess."

The three couples stood off to the side, obviously fuming but doing their best to hide it. They waved half-heartedly to the crowd. Sabrina was sure their "generous donations" were little more than bribes to keep them out of prison. Only a few days earlier the Grimms had discovered that these "wealthy donors" had gotten rich selling their Everafter children to Rumpelstiltskin.

"Some people asked me, 'Mayor Charming, what's the big deal? There are only a few Everafter children in this town. Why make all the fuss?' Well, I'll tell you why I'm making a fuss. Because you people elected me to make a fuss!"

He was again met with wild applause.

"The new school will have separate, exclusive classes for Everafter children that will teach our heritage, traditions, and values. It will feature a cafeteria offering lunches that meet the special dietary needs of our unique offspring. And lastly, it will be named after one of our own. From this day forward the children of Ferryport Landing, whether human or Everafter, will learn in a school named after the most famous Everafter of all time. Ladies and gentleman I proudly present to you Ferryport Landing's answer to the call of the future . . ."

Mr. Seven tugged on a large curtain behind the mayor. It fell to the floor, revealing a banner that read WILLIAM CHARMING ELEMENTARY. Below it was a huge bronze statue of the mayor standing with his chest puffed out and a wide grin on his face. Several frightened-looking children crouched at his feet, gazing up at him as if he were their only hope for survival.

The room was silent; then the grumbling began. Only Mr. Seven clapped, and he did it desperately, as if he feared for his job.

Suddenly, Sabrina was shoved from behind. A group of people were forcing their way through the crowd and up to the podium. A chubby woman wearing a long red dress and a golden crown climbed up on the stage and snatched the microphone out of the mayor's hand. Her face was covered in white powder and a little black birthmark had been drawn on her right cheek. Beside her was a small army of men in colorful uniforms. When Sabrina examined them more closely, she was shocked to discover their bodies were actually playing cards. The Queen of Hearts had arrived.

"I don't see any cause to celebrate," the queen said. "Having to rebuild this school is an unacceptable waste of taxpayer money and you, Mayor Charming, are to blame!"

Charming was startled but quickly recovered, and smiled widely at the irate woman. "Mrs. Heart, we're not here to debate policy. We're here to dedicate this wonderful new school to the youth of this town."

Mr. Seven clapped again, alone.

"The school wouldn't have had to be rebuilt if it weren't for you," the queen said as she turned to the crowd. "Everafters of Ferryport Landing, this sorry excuse for a mayor has let us down once again. In the last month we've had a giant run amok and cause property damage that has yet to be repaired. Our police force has been reduced to one pig, and public services, utilities, and infrastructure have fallen to the wayside. Four days ago, a perfectly good elementary school was blown to smithereens, and *you* are footing the bill. This man is completely incompetent."

"What's *incompetent* mean?" Daphne asked.

"It means he's not good at his job," Sabrina replied.

"Ferryport Landing has been in a bit of a budget crisis of late," the mayor said, looking defensive. "I have done the best I could with the resources at hand."

"Is that good enough for us?" the queen cried. Several people in the audience grumbled. A few even shouted "No!"

"No, it's not good enough!" the queen shouted. "But people, you don't even know the worst of it. Mayor Charming laid off two thirds of the police force so he could deputize the Grimms!"

A gasp went through the crowd.

"That's not exactly what happened," Charming said, smiling with gritted teeth.

"So you didn't deputize the Grimms?"

"Well, yes I did," the mayor said, as another gasp ran through the audience. "We were having an emergency. Rumpelstiltskin was going to . . . he built tunnels . . . the Grimms have special talents . . ." Charming was obviously rattled.

"So, now the only people who can solve Everafter problems are humans? You heard it yourself, folks. Your elected leader thinks that we can't govern ourselves, that we need help from humans, and not just any humans," the queen raged, "but the family that is responsible for our imprisonment!" She turned and pointed an ugly finger right at Granny Relda and the girls, "The Grimms!"

Sabrina gasped. Never had she had so much rage aimed at her and her family. She'd gotten used to knowing that most people in the town disliked them, but the queen's anger was rabid, and worse, it was infecting the crowd. Everywhere she looked furious eyes stared back at them. Instinctively, Sabrina stepped forward, putting herself between the crowd and her family.

"Mrs. Heart, I won't have you stand up here and tell this crowd that I'm a fan of the Grimms," Charming said. "No one despises that family more than I do!"

"Hey!" Daphne shouted. "We can hear you, ya know!"

The queen continued to rant. "Who knows how much influence Relda and her brood have over the mayor's office? Are they making our laws, too? I think it's time for a change. I think it's time for a new vision. We don't need a person who squanders the community's money and betrays its citizens by dealing with the Grimms. I for one have had enough!"

The words were so hateful that Sabrina jumped back in shock. Even Granny looked stunned by their ferocity.

"Today I'm announcing my candidacy for mayor of Ferryport Landing!" the Queen of Hearts declared. "And let me introduce you to the man who will become Ferryport Landing's new sheriff once I'm elected. He's a man of integrity—a man with centuries of experience—a man with a *legitimate* and *respected* career in law enforcement. Ladies and gentleman, allow me to introduce you to Sheriff Nottingham!"

A tall, broad-shouldered man with a handlebar mustache and long curly, black hair climbed to the stage. Despite a profound limp in his right leg, he was all aggression, from the deadly sneer on his lips to the long scar on his cheek to the clenched fists at his side. He looked at the crowd, unable at first to hide his disgust with all of them, and then forced an insincere smile to his face.

Several people cheered. "Maybe we should go," Granny Relda said to the girls.

"I agree," someone said. "Why are you even here? This celebration is for Everafters." The family spun around and saw a large group of Munchkins gathering nearby. Their leader's eyes flared with rage.

"I have as much right to be here as you do," Granny Relda replied tartly. "My family has been here as long as any Everafter."

"It'ssss your fault we're trapped here in thissss town," an enormous boa constrictor said as it slithered along the floor toward the Grimms.

An old witch hobbled toward them pointing her gnarly finger at the family. "Charming has been giving you Grimms a free ride for far too long. The queen is right. It's time for a change."

A small crowd of beasties, hobgoblins, and elves formed a tight circle around the family, cutting off their escape and any chance of help from friendly Everafters. "We've had enough!" a crow as big as a dog squawked. "The only thing that has kept you safe until now is the Big Bad Wolf. Now that your mongrel is dead and gone, what will you do?"

Daphne grabbed Puck's arm. "Do something!"

"Sorry, marshmallow. I told you. I'm back to being sinister."

Sabrina grabbed her sister's arm. "Leave him alone. He doesn't care about anyone but himself."

Daphne pulled away from Sabrina and faced Puck again. "Well, if we get killed you'll have no one to annoy all day long."

The boy cocked a curious eyebrow and nodded his head. His wings spread and he drew his sword.

"Back off you filthy trash-muncher!" he said to the crow. "The Grimms are mine to torment. Take another step and you'll be wishing the Wolf were still alive."

A cyclops stepped forward and cracked his knuckles. "Boy, I will pound you into pudding."

"You dare mock me!" Puck fumed as his arms morphed into those of a gorilla's. He pulled back and hit the cyclops right in the belly, sending him flying backward. The monster knocked Everafters over like bowling pins.

"Who's next?" the boy crowed. "Who thinks they can take on the Trickster King?"

Just then, a small, angry old man standing nearby began to grow in size. His clothing ripped, exposing a sickening green skin underneath. His cane morphed into an ugly, blood-smeared club that was nearly as big as the cyclops Puck had just flattened. He was a troll and the largest one Sabrina had ever seen. Worse, he was the angriest one she'd ever seen, too.

Everafters scattered in all directions as he stepped through the crowd.

"Come here, meat!" he growled.

"You are about to suffer one of the worst beatings of your life, troll," Puck said without flinching. "Run while you can. The Prince of Faerie isn't some billy goat you can scare off your bridge."

"Fairy, I'm going to rip you limb from limb and suck on your bones!" the troll roared.

"You don't know how many times I hear that in a day," Puck said. He swung his sword around and smacked the troll in the belly, with little effect. The monster looked more annoyed than hurt. With lightning-fast reflexes the brute lunged forward and knocked Puck to the ground, then sat hunched over the boy, flashing his horrible drool-dripping teeth. His neck muscles clenched as he prepared to feast on the boy. But suddenly there was a popping sound and Sabrina looked up to see a man materialize from thin air high above the gymnasium floor. He fell hard and fast, landing on top of the troll. The creature grunted with surprise, then bucked and kicked as he tried to remove his unwanted passenger, but the strange man held on. He reached into his overcoat and removed a small ring that he slipped onto his finger. He said a few unintelligible words and a cloud of black smoke swirled around the monster's head, blinding him.

"That's just about enough, Howard!" the stranger shouted at the troll. "Now, calm down or I'm going to get rough!"

The troll stumbled around, unable to see. He inadvertently knocked over the statue of Charming and it fell to the ground. Its head broke off and rolled across the floor.

"Turn your magic off, sorcerer!" the troll cried.

"Are you going to be a good boy?" the stranger demanded.

Howard the troll nodded. "Yes!"

The man said a few more words in the odd language and the cloud of smoke surrounding the brute's head vanished.

"Now go home and stay there until you've learned some manners," the man said to the hulking figure. "What would your wife think of your behavior?"

The troll lowered his eyes in shame and, along with several other Everafters, exited the gymnasium.

Daphne grabbed Sabrina's hand. "That's the man from last night," she whispered. Sabrina eyed the stranger closely. Her sister was right. The lunatic who had attacked them the night before had just saved their lives. Now he rushed over to the family and took Granny Relda into his arms. Sabrina watched dumbfounded as he gave the old woman a huge hug and a kiss on the cheek.

"Are you OK, Mom?"

"Mom?" Sabrina, Daphne, and Puck cried at the same time.

"I'm fine, Jacob," Granny replied.

5

The man hugged Granny Relda tightly and lifted her off her feet.

"Jacob, put me down." She laughed. "I'm an old woman."

The man set her back down. "You're not so old," he said.

"You look so thin! And what happened to your nose? It's broken!"

The man shuffled his feet like a schoolboy who has been caught placing a tack on his teacher's seat.

"Jacob! What did you do?" Granny asked, trying to sound stern while wiping tears of joy from her cheeks.

"It was nothing—just a little misunderstanding with a frost giant in Nepal. I think it makes me look rugged."

Puck stepped between the two and shoved his sword under

the man's chin. "Step away from the old lady or I'll run you through."

"Puck, this is my son," Granny said, pulling the boy away.

"Your son!" the girls cried.

"Yes, your Uncle Jacob," the old woman said.

"Call me Uncle Jake," said the man, opening his arms for a hug the girls didn't deliver. Sabrina was stunned. For the second time in less than two months the sisters had been introduced to a family member who they hadn't known existed.

"Henry didn't tell them about me?" the man said, seeming to read the girls' minds.

"Henry didn't tell them about me, either," Granny Relda said.

"Well, I'm *finally* happy to meet you," said the man with a wink that told them he knew the previous night's encounter was a secret.

"You must be Daphne," he said. "You've got Hank's grin."

"Hank?" Daphne asked.

"That's what we used to call your dad when he was younger," Uncle Jake said turning to Sabrina. "And that means you're . . . Sabrina. I am curious. Is the mustache and goatee some kind of fad I am unaware of, or did you lose a bet?"

Sabrina scowled and pulled her scarf back up to her nose.

"Just kidding, peanut," the man said with a laugh.

"My name is Sabrina," she said.

"Sorry, I can't help but give people nicknames."

"I want a nickname!" Daphne cried.

"How about shortstop?" Uncle Jake said, reaching down and ruffling the little girl's hair. Daphne giggled like she'd just gotten a Christmas present.

"And this is Puck," Granny said. She had her hands on the boy's shoulders like he was one of her own.

"I didn't need your help," Puck grunted at Uncle Jake before he could say hello. "I had everything under control."

Uncle Jake laughed. "Listen kid, you were knee-deep in trouble and you know it. Face it, some of the bad guys have to be handled by adults."

"Well, I'm a bad guy and you're an adult. Let's see how you handle me?" Puck retorted.

"Boys!" Granny shouted. "That's enough of this nonsense!"

Puck's face crinkled like he had just smelled a rotten egg. He huffed and shoved his sword back into his belt and then turned toward the exit.

"Where are you going?" Granny Relda asked.

"Away, old lady!" the boy snapped as he thrust the doors open. Before anyone could stop him, Puck was gone. Granny watched after him with worried eyes.

Sheriff Hamstead hobbled over to the group. His overworked belt had broken during the melee and he was having a terrible time keeping his pants up. "Relda, are you and the children OK?"

"Yes, yes, just a little shaken up. Was anyone hurt?"

"Not seriously," Hamstead answered as he looked around to be sure. "I've gotten the mayor, Mr. Seven, and Ms. White to safety and I'm asking everyone to go home."

"Of course," Granny Relda said.

"Sheriff Hamstead! How are you doing? It's been a long time," Uncle Jake said, hugging the policeman. Sabrina looked over at her sister. Apparently the "hugging thing" that Daphne was always doing ran in the family. Uncle Jake squeezed the man so tightly, Hamstead was unable to stop his pants from slipping down to his ankles, revealing boxer shorts with little pink cupids on them.

"Uh . . . do I know you, mister?" the sheriff said, with his face squished against Jake's chest.

Uncle Jake stepped back in surprise. "Know me? Of course you know me."

"Sheriff, this is my son Jacob," Granny Relda said.

Hamstead quickly pulled up his pants. "Relda, I didn't know you had another son," he said.

"Ernest, what are you talking about?" Uncle Jake said. "You

don't remember my brother and me? You caught us cutting school all the time. You took Hank and me down to the jail and locked us in a cell once. You told us that kids who skipped class had to go to prison and break rocks. It scared us half to death. We never cut again."

The sheriff studied Uncle Jake's face closely, but it was obvious to anyone that he didn't recognize the man. "Sorry, son. I have to chase down a lot of truants."

"But—"

Granny took her son by the sleeve and pulled him toward the exit before he could finish his sentence. "Let us know if you need any help, Sheriff."

She hustled the family outside and across the parking lot, where they found Mr. van Winkle sound asleep in his cab. Elvis had crawled into the front seat and was also snoring happily with his head resting on the old man's lap. The sack with the mozzarella-and-pepper sandwich had been torn open and its contents consumed. When Elvis let out a rather loud burp, Sabrina knew it wouldn't take a detective to figure out who had stolen the cab driver's lunch.

"You're not still using cars to get around, are you?" Uncle Jake said. "Why not use a flying carpet or something in the teleportation room? Mirror has all kinds of stuff!"

"I prefer to do some things the old-fashioned way," Granny said.

Uncle Jake rolled his eyes.

Granny Relda opened the car door and pushed down on the horn.

The cabbie jumped in his seat. "Sweet mother of pearl!" he shouted. "What? Is it over all ready?"

"We're ready to go."

Mr. van Winkle rubbed his tired eyes and looked down at Elvis. Then he noticed the remains of his lunch.

"This dog is a menace," he complained.

The big dog licked his lips with an expression that seemed to say, "Who? Me?"

"Elvis, that's not very nice," Granny said. "We'll stop on the way home and get you something to eat, Mr. van Winkle."

"And a cup of coffee," Sabrina grumbled as she climbed into the front seat next to the gassy dog.

• • •

By the time Mr. van Winkle pulled the cab into the driveway of the family's two-story yellow house, everyone was a nervous wreck. Granny shoved a handful of bills into the cabbie's hands.

"Thanks for the ride," the old woman said. "And Merry Christmas to you."

Mr. van Winkle seemed pleased with his tip. "Sure, lady. And remember, the next time you need fast, reliable, and friendly service, call me," he said as he shoved business cards into everyone's hands. "But next time the furball stays home."

Moments later he was gone.

"This place hasn't changed at all," Uncle Jake said as he marveled at the little house. "I bet there's still a dozen Frisbees on the roof."

"Things don't change much in Ferryport Landing," Granny said as she climbed the porch steps to the front door and began to unlock it.

"Wait a minute! I know something that's different. Why isn't the house decorated for the holidays?"

The old woman blushed as if she was ashamed.

"When we were kids, this place had so many lights on it you could probably see it from space," Uncle Jake told the girls. "The electric bill was so thick they had to spiral-bind it."

"We've been a bit busy lately," Granny Relda explained.

"Well, leave the decorating to me then," her son said as he reached into his pocket and took out a long, carved wand. "I'll have this place looking like the North Pole in no time."

"Jake, I absolutely forbid it," Granny Relda said, but Uncle Jake ignored her. He held the wand aloft and shouted, "Gimme some Christmas!"

A blinding ray of red-and-green light illuminated the yard. Within the beam Sabrina could see tiny particles moving and rearranging into solid objects that zipped across the lawn and grew in size. Suddenly, two enormous inflatable snowmen appeared in the center of the yard. A row of ten-foot candy canes lined the driveway all the way to the end. Red ribbons encircled the porch banisters and a mechanical Santa Claus in a shiny sleigh landed on top of the house. An odd, robotic "Ho, Ho, Ho!" blasted out of its mouth. Lines of multicolored blinking lights entwined every tree, bush, and shrub. Even poor Elvis found himself wrapped from head to toe in twinkling lights.

Daphne ran to a candy cane, sniffed it, and then gave it a lick. "Uh, hello! This is real!"

Granny rushed to Elvis's side and did her best to free him from his holiday-inspired bonds while Jake led the girls into the house.

"That takes care of the outside," he said. He handed the wand to Sabrina.

"Want to give it a try?"

Sabrina eyed the wand carefully. Just holding it sent a charge through her like nothing she had ever felt. This simple stick of wood packed a lot of power and Sabrina could feel it all the way down to her toes.

"What do I do?" she asked.

"Imagine how you want everything to look," Uncle Jake said as Granny finally entered the house. "And then ask for it.'"

Sabrina closed her eyes, nodded to herself, and then aimed the wand at the living room.

"Sabrina Grimm, I absolutely forbid it!" Granny cried, but she was too late again.

"Gimme some Christmas," Sabrina said, and the light blasted out of the wand. The rearranging particles twisted and turned into forms that eventually became a beautiful white-needled tree, covered in shiny bulbs and lights, showered in tinsel, strung with popcorn garlands, and topped with a gleaming angel. Mountains of presents were tucked underneath. A choo-choo train raced from room to room on a track and Bing Crosby crooned "White Christmas" from a stereo exactly like the one Sabrina and Daphne's parents had owned in New York City.

"It's just like home," Daphne cried happily.

"Jacob Alexander Grimm!" Granny fumed. She raced over to Sabrina and took the wand out of her hand. The little charge Sabrina had felt from the wand was gone and she immediately wished she could get it back.

"Oh, Mom, don't be a humbug," Uncle Jake said. "It's the girls' first Christmas in the house. It should be memorable."

"I wholeheartedly agree, but I don't think we need magic to do that," Granny said as she put the wand back in her son's hand. "One of the special things about Christmas is that the family decorates the house together."

"Says you! Why do something in days when you can do it in seconds?"

Granny shook her head as if to say she was disappointed that Uncle Jake didn't understand.

The morning slipped into afternoon and finally into evening as Uncle Jake told one hair-raising story after another of his many adventures. The girls hung on his every word; even Granny was fascinated with her son's tales and eventually decided to order pizza for dinner rather than miss another of Jake's stories while she was cooking.

"So how come we've never met you before?" Daphne asked as she helped herself to another slice with pepperoni.

"Well, I haven't been around in awhile. I've been traveling the world and getting into trouble," Uncle Jake said with a grin. "For a while I lived in Prague with Tom Thumb and then spent some time in India, Russia, Japan, Germany, and even Costa Rica, but lately I've been working with the Andersen triplets."

"Who are they?" Sabrina said.

"You don't know who the Andersen triplets are?" Uncle Jake said in a way that made Sabrina feel self-conscious.

"Henry chose to keep the children out of the loop when it came to the family business," Granny Relda said.

"All of it?"

The old woman nodded.

"Where do I start?" Uncle Jake said. "OK, you two are the sisters Grimm because you are descendants of the Brothers Grimm. The Andersen triplets are the descendants of Hans Christian Andersen."

"So they're fairy-tale detectives, too?" said Daphne.

"No, not exactly. They don't investigate mysteries. They hunt and collect magical items," Uncle Jake said as he retrieved the wand from his pocket. "That's how I got this bad boy. It's the Wand of Merlin. I found it at a garage sale in Athens, Ohio. The owner thought it was a back scratcher."

Granny frowned. "And I suppose that's how you suddenly just appeared out of thin air."

Uncle Jake grinned. He stood up, removed a jewel-encrusted belt from around his waist, and placed it on the table. "Nope, I used this."

"The Nome King's belt? Where did you get this?" Granny asked.

"That's not important. What's important is that I got it, though I think the batteries are dying. I wanted to pop in right next to the troll but this thing put me ten feet above him."

"Who's the Nome King?" Daphne said.

"You've never heard of the Nome King?"

The girls shook their heads. "Dad didn't tell us anything. Didn't we already cover this?" Daphne said.

"Henry forbid them from reading fairy tales, too," Granny Relda explained.

"He what? That's crazy. OK, the Nome King is from the Oz books—*Ozma of Oz* if I'm correct—the third of Baum's histories. The Nome King was the ruler of an underground kingdom underneath a land called Ev that was across the desert from Oz. I hear it's all condos and golf courses now. Anyway, Dorothy Gale washed up on the beach there after she fell off a boat."

"Dorothy is a little accident-prone," Granny said, rolling her eyes.

"I met her about a year ago. She's a tornado chaser in Kansas. She's got nerves of steel. Anyway, Dorothy managed to get the belt away from the little man and it helped her get back to Kansas. It works just like the magic slippers. Imagine yourself somewhere and—bingo-bango!—you're there!"

"And it runs on batteries?" Sabrina said, not quite sure if her uncle was pulling her leg.

"Yeah, twelve of the big ones and they get drained pretty fast. It costs me almost thirty bucks every time I use this thing—even if it's just to pop up across the street."

"You could always walk," Granny muttered.

"You haven't changed a bit, have you?" Uncle Jake said with a laugh. "Still antimagic?"

"I'm not antimagic. I just think it makes people lazy and is very addictive. Before you know it, all you can think about is magic rings and wands and flying carpets."

"That reminds me of a funny story. Once Hank and I got the magic carpet out and—"

"Why don't we use the belt to find Mom and Dad?" Sabrina interrupted.

"Sorry, 'Brina," Uncle Jake said. "You have to know an exact location. But don't worry, Jake Grimm is on the case. We're going to get your parents home in no time. That's why I came back to town."

Sabrina grinned from ear to ear.

"It's getting late and we all need our rest," Granny said. "We can start back up on this trip down memory lane in the morning."

"What about Puck?" Daphne said, tossing a slice of pizza into the air for Elvis to catch in his hungry jaws.

"He'll be back when he's ready. The boy has slept outside most of his life. He'll be fine," the old woman assured them. "Jacob, I'll get some blankets and a pillow for you. You can sleep on the couch tonight."

"Why can't I sleep in my own room?" Uncle Jake complained.

"It's not your room anymore," the old woman said. "I gave it to Mirror after you left."

"You gave my room to the magic mirror?" Jake cried. "He doesn't need his own room. You could put him in a closet and he wouldn't care."

"Come along, *lieblings*," the old woman said, ignoring her son's complaint.

The girls climbed the stairs to bed, stopping in the bathroom to wash their faces and hands, and brush their teeth. Daphne slipped into her favorite pair of footy pajamas, then helped Sabrina put on an old T-shirt and flannel pajama bottoms. The sisters crawled into bed.

"Can you believe we have an uncle?" Daphne said.

"I can believe just about anything with this family," Sabrina answered. "I wonder why Dad never told us about him."

"I guess he was trying to protect us from all of this, but..."

"But what?"

Daphne pointed at a photo hanging on the wall. In it, two boys sat on a steep hill overlooking the Hudson River. Sabrina knew one of the boys was her father and had always assumed the other was a childhood friend. Looking at the second boy closely, she saw the now familiar quirky grin. "Well, there's only this one picture of Uncle Jake in the whole house."

"So?"

"So that's not how a mom acts," Daphne said. "Think about all the pictures Mom took of us. They were all over the apartment. Since we moved here, Granny's taken at least a million of us. There are pictures of Mom and Dad, Grandpa, and Mr. Canis all over the place. There's three dozen of Elvis in the living room alone. Why not Uncle Jake?"

"That is a little odd," Sabrina said.

"And why isn't there a journal for Uncle Jake on the shelves? It seems like Granny was trying to hide him from us," Daphne said. "She went to a lot of trouble to make it seem like he was never born."

• • •

A tap on the window woke Sabrina. Unsure if she had imagined it, she lay in bed until she heard it again. *Puck! He lost his keys and needs me to let him in the house.* She climbed out from under her blankets and went to the window. When she peered out she saw her father and mother standing in the yard below. Sabrina tried to open the window but couldn't, quickly remembering that Mr. Canis had nailed it shut for their protection shortly after the girls arrived.

"Daphne! Wake up!" Sabrina shouted but the little girl was sound asleep. From past experience, Sabrina knew that sometimes her sister was impossible to wake, so she raced out of the room alone.

Down the stairs she went, two at a time. Without bothering to put on shoes or a coat, she darted out the front door and around to the side of the house.

"Mom! Dad!" she cried, as she turned the corner and ran smack into something enormous. She fell to the cold ground and looked up. The Jabberwocky was standing over her. On each of its disgusting hands was a puppet, one sewn to resemble a man with blond hair and the other a woman with raven locks, crudely similar to her parents. Sitting on the beast's shoulders was Little Red Riding Hood.

Sabrina crawled backward across the frozen grass, desperate to get away. The Jabberwocky tossed its puppets aside. Reaching down, it snatched Sabrina off the ground and dragged her close to its thousand gnashing teeth. Red Riding Hood leaned down and smiled as if they were great friends.

"I want to play house," the little girl said. "And when I want something, I get it."

That's when Sabrina woke up.

Her pajamas were soaked with sweat and her head was pounding. She looked around the bedroom to double check that she was indeed awake and fought the urge to cry.

She awkwardly crawled out of bed and tiptoed across the floor, then slipped into the hallway. She crept down the steps and into the living room where her uncle was sleeping on the couch. His overcoat, with its hundreds of pockets, was draped over the back. Sabrina knew that Little Red Riding Hood's medical file was in one of them. She *could* wait for her uncle to wake, but time was wasting. She stepped softly to the couch and lifted the long coat. She quickly found the file, but before she could grab it and hurry back upstairs, Uncle Jake's hand seized her arm.

"You're good," he said.

"Let me go," Sabrina said.

"You missed the creaky beam on the bottom step. I could never get around that. Your grandmother caught your father and me more times than I can count because of that last step," he said.

Sabrina tried to pull away from his grasp but he held on.

"You could have just asked for it," he continued. Her uncle reached into his overcoat and removed Red Riding Hood's rolled-up medical file. He released Sabrina's arm and handed her the file.

"I couldn't trust you'd give it to me." Sabrina tried to explain. "Granny keeps telling me all this Red Riding Hood stuff is too dangerous. I figured you'd just say the same."

"Now I know your father never told you anything about me. I love my mom, but we rarely agree on anything," Uncle Jake said with a laugh. "Listen, your grandmother's right. These people who took your parents are dangerous, but we still have to face them to get Henry and Veronica home. I think we should do it together. I figure that way we can get both of them home a lot faster."

Faster was what Sabrina wanted. She nodded and Uncle Jake leaped off the couch. "Good, let's get started. But first we need a little magic." He led her into the kitchen and flipped on the light, then searched through every cabinet until he finally found what he wanted—a can of coffee. "Ah, liquid magic," he said with a grin.

Sabrina's mom and dad were coffee fanatics. They drank it morning, noon, and night. She'd seen her mother wait in hour-long lines and pay more than five bucks for a cup of foam she called a latte. When her father was late for work, he drank a mug of coffee in the shower. Sabrina had once asked for a sip but her dad had refused. "It's not good for a kid," he'd said, as he swallowed a big gulp. "It'll stunt your growth."

Uncle Jake found some coffee filters in a drawer and an ancient instruction manual for the coffee maker. In no time, the smell of fresh roast was filling the room and his magical elixir was dripping into the pot. When the coffee was finished, he poured out two mugs worth and handed one to Sabrina.

She took a sip. It was bitter and gross and tasted a lot like mud. She spit it out into the sink, turned on the faucet, and stuck her mouth under the cool water to wash out the taste.

"When you get older, you'll love it," her uncle said.

"If this is what I have to look forward to when I'm older, I think I'll stay eleven."

"You know, I wanted to apologize about the other night," Uncle Jake said. "But you kids wouldn't give me a chance to explain who I was."

"We generally don't give the benefit of the doubt to weirdos hanging around in burnt-out buildings," Sabrina said.

"Takes one to know one." Uncle Jake laughed. He opened the sugar bowl and spooned three heaping helpings into Sabrina's mug. "This will kill the bitterness."

Sabrina stirred the concoction and took another sip. It *was* better. She nodded at her uncle and he smiled. He led her into the dining room and they both sat down. Sabrina set Red Riding Hood's medical file on the table and her uncle opened it.

"I looked through this earlier but I didn't understand much of it. There's a lot of medical mumbo jumbo in here. But I have discovered one thing," Uncle Jake said.

"What's that?"

"Little Red Riding Hood is a certifiable loony tune."

Sabrina frowned. "I could have told you that."

Uncle Jake grinned. "I also found this," he said, passing her a yellowing sheet with typing on it. "The little girl's history."

Little Red Riding Hood's medical history read much like her famous fairy-tale story. She was sent into the woods by her mother to take her old grandmother some food. Along the way she met a horrible beast she described as a wolf. When she got to the house she saw what she thought was her grandmother sitting in bed. Her grandmother had actually been killed and eaten by the wolf. The beast had put on her grandmother's clothing to fool the child. Just before the wolf could kill Little Red Riding Hood as well, the child discovered the disguise and ran into the woods. There she found a woodcutter who hunted the wolf, cut him open, and shoved rocks into his belly. Then

this woodcutter tossed the wolf's body into the river where it sank to the bottom. The man took the girl back to the village in hopes of returning her to her family, but her parents were never found. It was her doctors' belief that Red Riding Hood's mind was severely distressed by the events, causing her to have a break with reality. The doctors had had no success reaching her and medications were equally unsuccessful.

"The Big Bad Wolf made her crazy," Sabrina said. She thought of Mr. Canis. The old man hadn't been capable of such brutality, but his alter ego, the Wolf, was pure evil. For a moment, Sabrina felt sorry for Red Riding Hood.

"That's what her doctors thought, too, but you don't need a medical degree to figure that out. All you have to do is look at these."

He handed her a stack of papers. Sabrina flipped through them. The first few were finger paintings of a family. There was a mother and a father holding a baby, a kitten, a grandmother, and a ferocious-looking dog. As Sabrina flipped through them she found that the colors the girl used were less and less varied. The paintings got darker and darker until eventually they were entirely black and red. Looking at them made Sabrina queasy.

"That's her family," Uncle Jake said. "There's dozens more."

"She's a little obsessed," Sabrina muttered.

"No, she's a lot obsessed. She's never gotten over her loss."

"But it happened hundreds of years ago. Her grandmother is dead. Her mom and dad disappeared."

"Not in her mind," Uncle Jake said. "I think she's collecting a new family to replace the one she lost."

Sabrina felt her blood stop running in her veins. "She's got Mom and Dad and when I confronted her she said something about having a baby brother."

"Exactly," Uncle Jake said, pointing to the mother, father, and baby in the drawings.

"She said something else," Sabrina went on. "She said, 'Tell grandma and the puppy I'll see them soon. Then we can all play house.'"

"She needs them, too. And who do we know around here who is a grandma with a dog?'

Sabrina nearly cried out. *Granny Relda!*

Uncle Jake took the paintings and put them back into the file. "It doesn't tell us where Red Riding Hood may have gone, but at least we know where she's headed. We're all going to have to be prepared to defend your grandmother if that girl and her freaky pet show up."

"I don't know what kind of help I'm going to be," Sabrina said as she gestured to her broken arm.

"Oh, I'll fix that," Uncle Jake said rushing into the living room and returning with his overcoat. He sat back down and started rifling through its pockets.

"Where did I put it?" he mumbled to himself. He took a bottle out of his coat. Apparently it wasn't what he was looking for and he tossed it aside. Sabrina peered down at it. The label said, EVIL EYE DROPS. A small tube labeled CURSE-B-GONE and then a tub of cream called WITCH HAZEL REPELLENT were also rejected.

"Here it is," Uncle Jake said, finally pulling out a small round tin and handing it to Sabrina. She glanced at the label. SATIN SURGEON'S SALVE—NOW WITH A LEMONY-FRESH SCENT!

"What's Satin Surgeon's Salve?" Sabrina asked as she popped the lid off. Inside was an icky black ointment that smelled like backed-up sewage. It made her gag.

"You've never heard of this stuff?" Uncle Jake said as if exasperated. "I can't believe Henry didn't even teach you the basics. Andrew Lang wrote about this in *The Olive Fairy Book*. The story is about a princess who saved the life of the man she loved. The rumor is she got the salve from Cupid himself."

"What's in this stuff?" Sabrina said as she pinched her nose.

"You don't want to know." Uncle Jake took the tin and dipped his fingers into the rancid glop, which he rubbed over

Sabrina's hand. The vile stuff felt as bad as it smelled. Her head started spinning and an odd sensation ran up and down her arm, as if someone had poured an icy-cold glass of water into her cast. After a few seconds, the tingling stopped. Unfortunately the smell remained.

"Feel better?" Uncle Jake said.

Sabrina wasn't sure. The constant pain in her arm was gone. She tried to move her fingers and found they wiggled easily. Uncle Jake rushed into the kitchen, opened a drawer, and rummaged through it, then ran back to Sabrina. In his hand was a pair of heavy kitchen scissors.

"The proof is in the pudding," he said and he started cutting her plaster cast off. He removed it and tossed it to the floor. "Give that arm a try."

Sabrina turned her arm slowly. She quickly realized she could move it in any direction she wanted. It felt fine. In fact, it felt better than it ever had. "It worked!" she cried.

"Of course it worked. It's magic. I just can't understand why my mother wouldn't have done this for you already. Mirror's got rooms of this stuff. Haven't you and your sister come across the pharmacy in the Hall of Wonders, yet?"

"I'm not allowed in the Hall of Wonders." Sabrina sighed.

"You're kidding."

"No, I'm not. I was swiping Granny's keys and making copies without her permission. I've been banned."

"Wait! You don't have your own set of keys?" Uncle Jake exclaimed. "How do you and Daphne learn about all the stuff inside?"

"We don't. Granny says we're not ready."

"Not ready! You're practically over the hill! C'mon." Uncle Jake grabbed her arm with one hand and his overcoat with the other and rushed up the steps. Once they got to the landing, they stopped at the door to Mirror's room, which Granny Relda always kept locked. Uncle Jake searched his pockets and quickly found a set of keys as large and impressive as the old woman's.

"I don't know about this," Sabrina whispered as he unlocked the door. "She really doesn't want me in there. When she found out what I had done, she went ballistic."

"Yeah, she does that a lot," Uncle Jake said as he opened the door. The two stepped inside and closed the door behind them.

Just then, a blinding bolt of lightning struck inches from their feet, leaving a black smoldering spot on the hardwood floor.

"Who dares invade my sanctuary?" a horrible voice bellowed. Sabrina jumped back. A menacing face appeared in the mirror

hanging on the opposite wall. It was filled with anger and power and a thunderstorm raged behind it.

"That was a little close, don't you think?" Sabrina complained, walking right up to the mirror.

"Starfish? I'm so sorry," the face said, softening. "I thought I was being attacked by a pirate. Hang on for a second."

The face vanished and when it came back it was wearing a pair of glasses with smart tortoiseshell frames.

"Oh, I *am* being attacked by a pirate," Mirror said, eyeing the girl's black-marker goatee and mustache closely. "Would it be safe to say that Puck had something to do with this particular accessory?"

Sabrina nodded.

"He's just delightful, isn't he?" Mirror replied sarcastically.

"Mirror?" Jake said.

Mirror turned and focused his eyes on Uncle Jake. A huge grin appeared on his face. "Well, look what the cat dragged in!" he cried.

Jake rushed forward and did something most people would find impossible—he stepped into the reflection and vanished. Sabrina wasn't surprised in the least, though. After all, the mirror was more than just a reflective surface. It was also a doorway, and she followed her uncle through it.

On the other side was an enormous, barrel-vaulted hallway that reminded her of Grand Central Station in New York City. The ceiling was held up by massive marble columns. Rows and rows of arched doorways lined both walls. Each led to different rooms, all packed with magical and otherworldly items. Granny called it "the world's largest walk-in closet." The man known as Mirror called it "the Hall of Wonders" and it was where he lived.

Jake hugged the little man tightly, causing him to drop a small book he was carrying. "It's good to see you, Mirror."

"It's good to be seen," Mirror said as he squirmed to break from the younger man's embrace.

"You're looking great," Uncle Jake said, finally releasing him.

"Well, I do what I can. I drink a lot of water, and of course my Pilates instructor has really helped."

Sabrina leaned down and picked up the man's book. It was a paperback collection of word games like crosswords and jumbles.

"What's this?" she asked.

"Oh, Relda picked it up for me at the supermarket. She said she thought it might help pass the time. I could just kill her. I'm addicted to it now. Next time you see her, tell her to get me some more of them," Mirror said, turning his attention back to Uncle Jake. "What's with the family reunion, Jakey?"

"Jabberwocky stuff," the younger man said, gravely.

"Yes, I heard it was back," Mirror said, turning to Sabrina. "That thing has been running loose for far too long. Unfortunately, there's nothing in any of these rooms that can stop it."

"Oh, I knew that." Uncle Jake sniffed. "No, the reason we're here is I've got a niece in desperate need of a little experience with magic stuff."

"I smell trouble," Mirror warned.

"I think that's the salve," Sabrina replied. The noxious medicine was still making her feel nauseated.

"Mirror! Don't worry," Uncle Jake said flashing his quirky grin. He handed the little man his huge set of keys. "Let's start with some hats."

"As you wish," Mirror replied. He turned and led them down the hallway.

Lining the walls were doors of all shapes and sizes. Some were made of metal, others wood, and one looked as if it was made of ice. Each door had a little bronze plaque that told what was behind it. POISONED SPINNING WHEELS, TREE SPRITES, CRYSTAL BALLS, LOVE POTIONS, ALL THE KING'S HORSES (right next to ALL THE KING'S MEN). The doors went on and on down a hallway that seemed to go on forever. Sabrina wondered if anyone had ever walked to the end or even if there was an end.

"Relda will not be pleased," Mirror commented, as he escorted them down the hall.

"Mom is just being stubborn. The girls need to know what's in these rooms. Dad made sure that Hank and I knew how to use this stuff and it got us out of a lot of close calls."

"It also got you *into* a lot of close calls, as I remember it," Mirror said.

Uncle Jake ignored the comment and turned to Sabrina. "Your dad and I spent hours in here every day, learning how the wands worked, testing out the magic shoes, learning how to fight with the swords and armor, and learning to use the translation spells so we could speak with birds, fish, and forest animals. These rooms are filled with useful stuff."

Mirror stopped at a door with a plaque that read HATS, HELMETS, BEANIES, ETC. He found the key for the lock and opened the door. He stepped inside and soon returned with a metal helmet that had small antlers mounted on each side.

"Good choice," Uncle Jake said. "The Midas Crown."

"What does it do?" Sabrina asked, as her uncle placed it on her head.

"It makes you strong. Try to pick me up," Uncle Jake said.

"But you're three times my size."

"Try it!"

Sabrina reached over and grabbed her uncle by the shirt and lifted with all her strength. It was more than she needed. Uncle Jake went flying into the air and plummeted back into Sabrina's arms. His landing was awkward but he wasn't hurt.

"Oh, man am I going to have fun with this!" Sabrina cried as she felt the power of the helmet course through her limbs.

"Sabrina, wait for me in the hall," a voice said behind them. Sabrina turned and saw Granny Relda. The old woman's face was red with anger. Daphne stood next to her with sleepy eyes and a confused expression.

"Busted," Uncle Jake whispered.

"I want everyone out of here right this instant," Granny Relda demanded, fixing her eyes on Sabrina, showing the girl how disappointed she was.

"Hey! Your arm is healed," Daphne said.

"I suppose you used magic," Granny said.

"It was silly to have her in pain," Uncle Jake said. "Why wait three months when it could be perfectly fine today?"

"And what is the cost of that, Jacob?"

"I don't understand the question."

"There is a cost with magic. There is always a cost."

"There's no cost. Her arm is healed," Uncle Jake said defensively. "The magic asked for nothing in return."

"The magic most certainly asked for something. It asked for experience. Sabrina broke her arm doing something I told her not to do. The healing is her experience in learning about the consequences of the choices she makes. Sure, it is easier to wave a wand or rub some magic medicine over our injuries. It's always easier. But what do we learn? How will Sabrina know her limitations?"

"Mom, you talk as if Sabrina and Daphne were normal little girls," Jake replied. "But they are not. They are Grimms and their lives are going to be difficult. Let the rest of the children learn about limitations. They don't have a Jabberwocky and a certifiable nutcase like Red Riding Hood chasing their family. The girls have to learn to fight. If they knew how to use some of the stuff you have locked up in here, Sabrina might not have gotten hurt in the first place. They need to be trained like Hank and I were. Dad had us exploring these rooms when we were five years old and—"

"Your father was wrong," Granny Relda said. "The girls will explore the mirror's rooms when I say they are ready. Until then, the best lesson I can teach them is that magic always has a price!"

"That's ridiculous!" her son complained.

"Is it Jake? Is it still so hard to see after everything that has happened? Your father is dead because . . ." Granny Relda stopped in mid sentence and there was a long silence between the two.

"You don't have to tell me why Dad is dead," Uncle Jake said. "I'm the one who killed him."

"Jake, I didn't mean . . ."

But Uncle Jake didn't let her finish. He turned, walked back down the hallway, and disappeared through the portal.

6

abrina and Daphne followed their grandmother into their bedroom. She said nothing, only pointed at the bed. It spoke volumes, and the girls crawled in.

"Did Uncle Jake really kill Grandpa?" Daphne asked, but the old woman just shook her head. Sabrina wasn't sure if her grandmother was saying no to the question or just didn't want to talk about it.

"I think Uncle Jake is right," Sabrina said. "When are you going to teach us how to use the magic in the Hall of Wonders?"

The old woman cringed slightly as if the question physically hurt her.

"We have plenty of time for that," she said.

"We don't have any time at all," Sabrina said. "Uncle Jake and

I discovered Red Riding Hood's plan. She's trying to rebuild her lost family. She's got Mom and Dad and some poor family's baby. Now she's coming after you."

Daphne gasped. "Is that true?"

"That's not going to happen," the old woman said, as she pulled the covers over the girls. "Nothing bad is going to happen to me."

"Can you guarantee that?" Sabrina said. "Because if you can't, the two of us would be left alone in this town, and you saw how angry everyone got at the school. If something did happen to you, would the two of us be able to protect ourselves?"

"Sabrina, stop!" Daphne demanded.

Sabrina's angry words rang in her own ears. It had been a heartless thing to say to her grandmother. She wished she could take it back.

The old woman looked stunned for a moment and then turned and exited the room without even a *good-night.*

"You know what? I have a question, Sabrina," Daphne said. "When are you going to stop acting like such a snot?"

"Daphne, you didn't see Red Riding Hood or the Jabberwocky," Sabrina grumbled. "I did, and Granny needs to take this seriously."

Daphne crossed her arms and huffed, then turned her back

on her sister. She pulled the pillow from underneath her and put it over her head to block out Sabrina's voice.

• • •

The next morning Sabrina woke early in hopes of having some time alone with Uncle Jake. Maybe they could go through the journals and look for any information about Red Riding Hood and the Jabberwocky she might have missed. Unfortunately, he was gone when Sabrina got downstairs. Instead, she found Granny Relda parked in her chair at the dining room table, sipping tea and writing in her own journal of fairy-tale accounts. When she saw Sabrina, she smiled as if the previous night's argument hadn't even occurred.

"I called the pharmacy to find out if there is anything we can do about the marker on your face," the old woman said. "Unfortunately, it looks as if only time will help. They assured me it will fade in a couple of days."

Sabrina scowled. *A couple of days!*

"What do you want for breakfast? I'll make you anything you want," the old woman said, but before Sabrina could answer, Uncle Jake burst into the house and set a bright-pink donut box on the table.

"I brought breakfast," he said as he walked around the table and planted a big kiss on his mother's cheek. "Hello, beautiful."

The old woman tried to keep a serious face but Sabrina could see Uncle Jake's charm was working on her. Soon she surrendered a grin. "Jake, the children need something healthy in the morning."

"What the girls need is to try these. I waited outside the Baker's shop for an hour to get them. He makes his donuts in the middle of the night and if you're there when he opens the shop at five a.m., you can get them while they're fresh and hot. You should have seen the line! It was around the block! Even the Butcher and the Candlestick Maker were there, and those three can't stand one another."

"Being lost at sea in an old tub can strain a friendship," Granny explained. She reached in and took out a glazed donut. When she took a bite, a huge smile came to her face. "Oh, these are heaven."

"I know," Uncle Jake said with a laugh. "I already had seven. I'm as hyper as a three-year-old so I hiked up to the top of Mount Taurus. Sabrina, you have to go up there with me some time. From the top, you can see the whole town."

"I was up there last week running from the Jabberwocky," Sabrina said sarcastically.

"Not quite the experience I had, huh? I had forgotten how beautiful Ferryport Landing is in winter!"

Yeah, all four blocks of it, Sabrina thought.

Daphne and Elvis entered the dining room. "I smell donuts!" Daphne said. Elvis's tongue was hanging out and dripping drool on the floor.

"Help yourself," Uncle Jake said, opening the lid of the box. Daphne reached inside and took two donuts.

"Two?" Uncle Jake said with a grin.

"One's for Elvis," the little girl explained, tossing one into the air. The Great Dane leaped up and snatched it in mid-flight. Sabrina wondered if he even tasted it before he swallowed it whole.

Daphne bit into hers first and sank into her chair in a dream-like state. "Oh . . . my . . . gosh," she mumbled with her mouth full.

"Sabrina?" Uncle Jake said, offering her a donut. She reached in and took one. They were warm and sticky. She took a bite and couldn't believe how delicious they were. It was like biting into pure happiness. It was all sugar and butter and love.

"Good, huh?" Jake said with a wink.

Sabrina nodded, afraid that if she opened her mouth to talk, some of the experience might escape.

"Mom, I got to thinking. You said yesterday that you and the girls have been pretty busy since they arrived. That's a real shame. This town has a few interesting spots, and I bet the girls would love to see some of the places where their dad and I used to hang out," Uncle Jake said.

"You mean the places you two used to get into trouble?" she said knowingly.

"Exactly!" He leaned over and kissed the old woman on the cheek again. "It'll be fun."

Granny nodded reluctantly.

"Great!" Uncle Jake said. He scooped up the pink box of donuts and raced out of the room. "I'm going to make sure Mirror gets one of these."

Just then there was a knock at the door.

"Who could that be this early in the morning?" Granny wondered aloud.

Sabrina shrugged and went to the door. When she opened it she was so surprised she nearly fell over. It was Mayor Charming. Snow White stepped out from behind him, followed by his personal assistant, Mr. Seven, who was wearing the biggest grin she had ever seen.

"Good morning, Sabrina. Is everyone home?" Snow White asked. "Billy has something he'd like to say to your family."

The mayor looked annoyed.

"Well, Captain, permission to come aboard?" he said sarcastically. Sabrina scowled and prepared to slam the door in his face when Granny came up behind her and invited everyone inside.

"Relda, I know it's early but I wanted to make sure you and the kids were OK after what happened yesterday," Ms. White said.

"Oh, no harm done," Granny said, flashing the mayor a disappointed look.

"Billy also has something important he wants to say to you and your family," the pretty teacher added. "But first, he has to get ready. Mr. Seven, if you would be so kind."

The little man reached into his jacket pocket and took out a small wad of paper. He unfolded it quickly and handed it to the mayor. Charming stared down at it with a scowl. Sabrina recognized it at once. It was a paper hat with the words I AM AN IDIOT written on it in big black letters. The Mayor often forced Mr. Seven to wear it.

"Do I have to?" Charming groaned.

"Billy Charming!" Ms. White scolded. "You promised!"

The mayor scowled and set the hat squarely on his head. Sabrina couldn't help but laugh, not so much at Charming's humiliation, but at the expression of triumphant satisfaction on the face of his diminutive sidekick, Mr. Seven. The dwarf looked as if he had just won the lottery.

"I'm sorry," Charming whispered.

"I don't think they heard you," Snow White said.

"Well then they all need hearing aids!" Charming snapped.

"Billy! You said you would do the right thing and if you don't I will never speak to you again," Ms. White threatened. "And you know I mean it. We went a few hundred years without saying even a word to each other!"

Mr. Seven stood off to the side snickering until Charming shot him a nasty look. The little man straightened up but went back to giggling as soon as the mayor turned his attention to the Grimms.

Charming sighed and his broad shoulders and chest seemed to deflate right before Sabrina's eyes. "I'm sorry I turned on your family at the dedication ceremony yesterday."

Sabrina was stunned. Charming had never apologized for anything as far as she knew, and she had two hundred years of family journals to prove it. She realized just how much power Snow White had over the mayor.

"But you have to understand, this family is like a cancer that is threatening to eat me alive," Charming continued. Ms. White gasped.

"Don't sugarcoat it, mayor. Tell us how you really feel," Sabrina grumbled.

"It's the election this weekend. I didn't expect to have an opponent this year. If the queen wasn't running, the only thing your presence would have given me was indigestion. But now that I might lose my job, the last thing I need is for the voters to start thinking that I'm aligned with the Grimms. There's no time for damage control like that. I hardly have time to buy the votes I need and hire people to stuff ballot boxes . . ."

Ms. White's eyes flared with anger. The look was not lost on the mayor.

"I mean, get my message of hope out to the community," he finished.

"And the last thing you need is to look like you're buddy-buddy with a bunch of lowlifes like us," Sabrina replied sarcastically.

"See, Snow? The child understands!" Charming cried happily. "This hasn't been a good year for the town; the giant caused millions in property damage, and replacing the school cost millions more. Ferryport Landing is flat broke. People are starting to think a change would be good and, trust me, the last thing you want is Mayor Heart running this town."

"I absolutely agree," Granny said. "If being anti-Grimm keeps you in office, then do what you have to do."

"Relda, I can't believe you," Snow White said with disappointment. "Do you know how hard it was to get him to apologize, and here you are encouraging the bad behavior?"

Just then, Uncle Jake came down the steps. "Ms. White, is that you?" he said, grinning from ear to ear.

Snow White looked at the young man with a curious expression. "I'm sorry. Have we met?"

"Ms. White, it's me, Jake Grimm. I was in your second grade class. My brother, Henry, was a year ahead of me."

"Your brother Henry?" Charming roared. "Relda, you never told me you had another son."

Uncle Jake looked at his mother suspiciously.

"Oh, I'm sure I mentioned it to you both," Granny said, ushering the visitors to the door. "Well, it was nice of you to drop by. We've got a busy day ahead of us. Good luck with the campaign, Mayor Charming."

"Every time I turn around there's another Grimm," Charming complained. "They're like cockroaches. This town is infested!"

"William Charming!" Snow White roared angrily as Granny closed the door in their faces.

"What did you do?" Uncle Jake said.

"I'm sure I don't know what you mean," Granny said to her

son as she turned and went back to the dining room. He chased after her.

"Mom, Hamstead doesn't remember me and he caught me and Hank skipping school probably a thousand times. Snow White doesn't remember me even though I wrote her a love letter every day until I turned eighteen. Charming doesn't remember me even though he threatened to have me arrested and had my face put on wanted posters all over town."

"People forget things, Jake," Granny said. "It has been twelve years."

"Mom, I'm not bragging when I say this, but let's be honest. I'm pretty hard to forget!"

Granny Relda looked around the room. Everyone was staring at her. Even Elvis cocked a curious eyebrow. The old woman shuffled her feet and stammered a bit until she finally decided what to say. "They don't remember you because I had the whole town sprayed with forgetful dust."

"You what?" Uncle Jake cried.

"When everyone found out what you did, there was chaos in the streets," Granny Relda said, as she cleaned up donut crumbs. "There was a mob outside my door for two weeks. People were getting hurt. It had to be done."

"What did you do?" the girls asked Uncle Jake.

Their uncle ignored the question. "So everyone has forgotten about me?"

"Not everyone," Granny continued. "Mirror and Mr. Canis remember you."

"Mom, Mr. Canis is dead," Uncle Jake reminded her. Granny flinched but then regained her composure.

"And Baba Yaga, of course," the old woman continued.

"Baba Yaga! Well that's just great! A mentally deranged cannibal who collects human bones still remembers me. How did I get so lucky?"

Uncle Jake left the room, snatched his overcoat from the hall closet, and opened the front door.

"Where are you going?" Granny Relda asked.

"To warm up the car," he called. "Get your coats, girls, and try not to forget all about me before you get outside." He stomped out and slammed the door behind him.

The girls stared at their grandmother but she wouldn't meet their eyes. "Puck snuck in late last night. Sabrina, run up and invite him along. I'm sure he's feeling a bit left out."

Sabrina wanted to know more about what her Uncle Jake had done, but Granny Relda had an increasingly familiar expression on her face. The old woman didn't want to talk.

• • •

The last person in the world whom Sabrina wanted to invite anywhere was Puck. She reluctantly climbed the steps and knocked on his door several times, but there was no answer. She pushed it open and inspected the ground for catapults, bear traps, secret levers, and stink bombs. The coast seemed clear, so she stepped inside.

She called out for the prankster but there was no response. After a couple more shouts she decided to give up. Just then there was a *pop!* A stream of fire and smoke rose high into the sky and exploded into a thousand multicolored lights, followed by an ear-shaking *boom!* Moments later, another trail of smoke whistled into the sky. The fireworks seemed to be coming from over a hill beyond the lagoon.

The path up the hill was littered with broken toys and melted army men. Shattered marbles, stretched-out Slinkys, and the heads of some Hungry Hungry Hippos were scattered everywhere. At the end of the path was a clearing where Sabrina found Puck sitting on a jewel-encrusted throne wearing his military medals. His chimpanzee army crowded around him, all reaching for a box of matches Puck held in his hands, as the boy lectured them on the art of war.

"Johnson, step up here," he said. One of the chimps stepped out of the crowd and approached the boy. "Johnson, the enemy is everywhere. You might even have to kill one of your own men if you were to discover that they were sympathetic to the enemy's cause. Could you take out your best friend if you had to?"

The chimp smiled widely, nodded, and clapped his hands.

"Johnson, you're a good soldier," Puck said. He lit a match and handed it to the furry creature. The lucky chimp raced over to a collection of fireworks of all shapes and sizes. Johnson lit the biggest red-and-white-striped rocket of the bunch and screamed with glee as it whistled into the air and exploded in the sky. When the lights and noise were gone, the chimps hopped up and down in front of Puck and begged to be the recipient of the next match.

"Sullivan, front and center!" Puck commanded. "Tell me the first rule of war."

The monkey screamed and stomped its feet.

"That's right Sullivan. Kill or be killed," Puck replied, handing him a match. Soon another rocket was flying overhead.

"What do you want?" Puck said when he spotted Sabrina.

"Somebody's in a bad mood," she taunted, stepping over several expired bottle rockets.

"I'm not in a bad mood," Puck said. "I'm busy turning these maggots into fighting machines."

The chimpanzees turned to him, baring teeth and screaming impatiently for another match. Puck's head suddenly morphed into that of a chimp as well and he hissed and spit at them. The chimps quieted and then went right back to begging for matches.

"The only thing keeping you busy is your pouting," Sabrina remarked.

"I'm not pouting."

"Well, something's wrong. There are donuts in the dining room. Normally you'd have already wolfed them all down and finished by licking the box."

"Who cares about donuts? I don't even like donuts," Puck said.

"You like everything. I've seen you eat Elvis's kibble right out of his bowl."

There was a long pause.

"Are they glazed?" he asked.

"Yes, Uncle Jake bought them," Sabrina said.

"I don't want anything from him."

"Why don't you like him?"

"He's hogging the old lady. Just cause he's her real son," Puck replied.

"She hasn't seen him in twelve years, Puck," Sabrina explained.

"Why do you care, anyway?"

"I don't!"

"Good!"

"Good!"

There was a long silence.

"If you must know, I've been insulted," Puck said.

"By who?"

"By all of you," Puck cried. "I have an impeccable reputation as a scoundrel. I have been banned by thousands of hamlets, hundreds of cities, dozens of countries, and three different dimensions. There are bounties on my head all over the planet and on a few planets you've never heard of. I'm Puck, the Trickster King. I'm the mean and nasty emperor of pranksters. I'm the boy hero to nations of snickering layabouts. My kingdom is the wrong side of the tracks!"

"So?"

Puck snarled. "So? *So?!* So, I threw it all away to protect this family and not one of you appreciates it. I'm ruined and you have all turned your back on me for *Uncle Jake*. He'll save the family, blah, blah, blah!"

"Oh, stop being such a baby. Of course we care about you. Everyone cares about you," Sabrina said.

"You care about me?"

"Don't let it go to your head, gasbag."

"You're in love with me! I knew it!"

"Gross!"

"You want me to be your boyfriend, don't you?" Puck taunted. His wings suddenly popped out of his back and he swooped over to Sabrina. Before she knew how to react, the boy kissed her on the lips. A million thoughts ran through Sabrina's head at once. Puck was annoying. He had dumped her in vats of disgusting glop. He'd put creepy crawlers in her bed. But the most awful thought of them all was the one about the kiss—it was nice.

The two separated and stared at each other for a long time. Puck grinned and broke the silence. "I believe the words you are searching for are *thank you.*"

And then Sabrina punched him in the belly.

Puck hunched over, gasping for breath.

"You try that again, you little freak, and you're going to need a dentist," Sabrina shouted. She turned and stomped back down the path. "We're going out with Uncle Jake. Granny says you have to go. We're waiting in the car!"

Sabrina found the door to Puck's room, opened it, and slammed it behind her. She leaned against the wood, feeling

hot embarrassment on her face. Ever since she had started noticing boys, she had dreamed about her first kiss. She had imagined it would occur on the beach or in a flower garden with a nice boy who really liked her. She had never once, not even in her worst nightmares, thought the boy would be Puck. She couldn't believe her first kiss had been from a dirty, smelly Everafter surrounded by a bunch of screaming chimpanzee pyromaniacs.

She rushed to the bathroom to see if her face looked different. Would anyone be able to tell what she and Puck had just done? She turned the water on, ran some soap over a washcloth, and scrubbed her face. When she was finished, her skin was as raw as when she had tried to scrub off Puck's mustache and goatee. She still looked flushed and embarrassed.

By the time Sabrina got back downstairs, Daphne was tapping her foot by the door.

"Where's Puck?" the little girl asked.

"He's coming," Sabrina said as she snatched her coat from the closet.

"Did you two kiss and make up?" Daphne asked.

Though she couldn't see it, Sabrina was sure her face was as red as a tomato. "C'mon, Uncle Jake is waiting," she said and hurried outside with Daphne at her heels.

Uncle Jake was leaning against the family's rusty old jalopy. It hadn't moved an inch since Mr. Canis had died.

Puck came out of the house to join them, and when the boy fairy got close enough, Uncle Jake extended his hand. "Glad to have you along, Puck," he said sincerely.

The boy sneered at the man and crawled into the backseat of the car. The girls followed and the ancient car's shock absorbers groaned with complaint. Seeing Uncle Jake behind the wheel where Mr. Canis usually sat was strange to Sabrina. But when Uncle Jake inserted the key something even stranger happened—the car didn't backfire. Every other time the girls had been in the car, it had started with an ear-shattering explosion that could be heard across town. Now it rumbled softly like a brand-new automobile. Sabrina saw her own surprise reflected in her sister's face.

"How did you do that?" Daphne said.

"I have a way with women," Uncle Jake said, caressing the dusty dashboard. "Besides, this is my car. I left it here when I skipped town. Your father and I got into a lot of trouble in this car."

He put the car in reverse and backed it out into the street, and soon they were tooling through the back roads of Ferryport Landing. What Sabrina had always thought of as the world's dullest town took on a whole new light when her uncle talked about it. Every mailbox, abandoned house, graffiti-covered bridge, and broken window had a story. The more the girls heard, the more it became clear that Uncle Jake and their straight-laced father had been first-class juvenile delinquents. As interesting as all the stories were, Sabrina found herself especially interested in the ones that had a magical element; the boys had cast a gigantic spell on the Three Blind Mice and watched them stagger around the town, they had poured a rusting potion onto the Tin Woodsman, and even found a way to give the Old Woman Who Lived in a Shoe and her thousand kids athlete's foot. Jake and her father had done it all.

Which made Puck's dislike of her uncle all the more puzzling. After all, the two had so much in common. Uncle Jake's stories were filled with mischief, but Puck was clearly unimpressed. He sat in the backseat, with his arms crossed, acting as if he weren't paying attention.

Sabrina and Daphne, on the other hand, had a wonderful time. Even the "A VOTE FOR HEART IS A VOTE FOR CHANGE" signs that had sprung up all over town couldn't cast a shadow on the trip.

After a couple hours of sightseeing, Uncle Jake made a turn that led up to the mountains. They drove for some time, then made a left on an abandoned gravel path and parked the car near a clearing.

"What are we doing here?" Daphne asked as everyone got out of the car.

"I have to admit that this walk down memory lane was all just a trick to get you girls out of the house," Uncle Jake replied, leading the children to the center of the open field. "Mom doesn't want you two messing with the stuff in the Hall of Wonders, but I have a few goodies of my own. I'm going to teach you to use some of them. Puck, would you like to learn something, too?"

Puck sneered. "I know all I'm gonna."

Uncle Jake dug in his pockets and produced his Wand of Merlin. He handed it to Daphne but she refused to take it.

Her uncle was surprised. "Wouldn't you like to have something that you can use to save your mom and dad and keep you and your sister safe? Your grandmother never has to know."

Daphne shook her head. "No, thank you."

Uncle Jake frowned and handed the wand to Sabrina. As soon as she touched it she felt the familiar charge run through her body. It was exhilarating.

"Looks like you're going to be the hero of this family. OK, the name of the game with a magic wand is control. You want to be able to aim and concentrate all at once 'cause the thing about monsters is they don't wait until you're ready. So every time you point this thing, know what you want or someone could get hurt."

Sabrina nodded, doing her best to avoid Daphne's disapproving glare.

"So you've seen how it works for garland and tinsel," Uncle Jake said. "Let's try something with a little more punch. Let's pretend those trees over there are the Jabberwocky. We need something really big to knock a Jabberwocky down. It could be anything, but let's try lightning. To get some lightning, think about the worst thunderstorm you've ever seen, a really scary one with fierce wind and rain."

Sabrina closed her eyes to imagine the scenario and immediately remembered the night after her parents had disappeared. There had been a terrible thunderstorm right outside of their apartment windows. The girls had slept in their mom and dad's bed, hoping they'd come home soon. They never did.

"Now aim and say, 'Gimme some lightning.'"

When Sabrina opened her eyes, that same thunderstorm was building in the sky above her. There was static energy in the air that caused the hair on her arms to rise. She felt supercharged, like she was filled with enough power to do anything she could imagine, like there was nothing that could hurt her. All of her fears and worries about Red Riding Hood and the Jabberwocky faded away and for the first time in a year and a half she felt calm and confident. It was a sensation so incredible she wondered if there was a way to feel it all the time.

In an instant, a bolt of lightning plummeted to the earth and crashed into the bank of trees. They disappeared for a moment in a flash of brilliant white light, which was followed by an earth-shaking *boom!* When it was over, the trees were cracked in half. Many were on fire.

"Nice shot, kiddo," Uncle Jake said. "I think you're a natural."

"Could lightning kill the Jabberwocky?" Sabrina asked. She imagined unleashing the wand's power on the monster and smiled.

"It won't kill it," Uncle Jake said. "But it would knock the ugly sucker off its feet, hopefully long enough to get your parents back."

Just then, one of Puck's pixie minions zipped across the field. It stopped at Puck's ear and buzzed excitedly. Puck's eyes lit up and his wings popped out of his back.

"There's someone in the woods watching us," he said, as he lifted off the ground.

"Looks like we're going to get a bit more practice," Uncle Jake said to the girls. "Come on!"

They all raced toward the forest and plunged into its thick

brush. Sabrina quickly caught a glimpse of someone running far ahead—a man. His speed was superhuman, and she watched him leap effortlessly over a downed tree. Before they could get a good look at him, he was gone.

"I'm going to follow him," Puck shouted, zipping into the woods.

"Be careful!" Sabrina shouted.

"And what would be the fun in that?" the boy said and disappeared into the forest.

"He's just dumb enough to confront that guy," Sabrina said.

"Naw, he wouldn't fight unless he had an audience. He'll be fine," Daphne said.

"I hate to admit it, but he's a lot like your dad and me," Uncle Jake said. "I can see why Mom and you love him so much."

"Love him? I don't love him. He's a pain in the butt!" Sabrina shouted, a bit louder than she meant to.

• • •

The group waited an hour and a half before they gave up on Puck. The boy could always fly home, so they got into the old car without him and cruised back down to the town. As they passed a diner, Uncle Jake slammed on the brakes and abruptly pulled into the parking lot.

"This place is the best!" he cried.

Sabrina had spotted the Blue Plate Special several times since they had moved to Ferryport Landing. It was right next door to the Ferryport Landing Post Office and had a neon sign of a grinning waitress holding a bright-blue tray of burgers and shakes. It was the kind of place her parents would have taken them to after a movie or a visit to the Central Park Zoo. Just looking at the sign made Sabrina's mouth water for the kind of old-fashioned egg cream her father had gotten her addicted to. That and a plate of cheese fries was a meal made for a king, even if it was made by witches and ogres. Granny had told her the Blue Plate Special diner employed a lot of Everafters.

The inside of the restaurant was decorated for the holiday season, with little Christmas trees painted on the windows and long strands of garland hanging from the ceiling. There were booths along a bank of windows, personal juke boxes at each table, and a counter at the front where people drank coffee and read the newspaper. A dessert case in the corner spun slowly, tempting diners with cheesecake dripping in strawberry sauce and chocolate parfaits. Overworked waitresses rushed from table to table, refilling coffees and shouting their odd diner-speak to the short-order cooks in the kitchen. The place smelled like hamburgers and mashed potatoes, and Sabrina knew everything would taste a little like chicken. She was in heaven.

At a table at the far end of the restaurant sat Mr. Swineheart and Mr. Boarman. They set down their coffee cups and waved to the group. The girls waved back and then slid into a booth near the door with Uncle Jake. They each snatched a menu from behind the ketchup caddy and scanned it eagerly.

"I swear I'm going to eat everything on this menu," Daphne said. "Who wants onion rings?"

Uncle Jake didn't respond. He gazed around the room, looking depressed.

"Uncle Jake?" Sabrina said.

"We used to come here when I was a kid. Hank and I would collect old soda bottles and take them to Tweedledee and Tweedledum's convenience store for the deposits. Then we'd head over here and drink chocolate malteds all day. This was our booth. That waitress at the door—she owns this place. We used to drive her nuts, but she doesn't even recognize me. That man at the counter—he's the Scarecrow. He runs the town library. I owe him probably forty dollars in late fees. Over in that booth at the end of the table is the Cheshire Cat—we once watched a pit bull chase him up a tree. The fire department had to come and get him down. He called us a couple of 'no-good hooligans' for laughing at him."

Sabrina turned around. The man Uncle Jake was referring to was studying his menu. He had the biggest eyes and grin Sabrina had ever seen outside of a cartoon.

"But I've been erased." Uncle Jake sighed.

"What did you do?" Sabrina said.

He shifted uncomfortably in his chair. "Something very, very stupid."

"How y'all doin'?" a waitress said as she bopped over to the table with a note pad and pencil in hand. She had a big out-of-date hairdo, bright-pink lipstick, and a name tag that read FARRAH. "What can I getcha?" she said, between chomps on her bubble gum.

"I'll have a grilled cheese with bacon and tomato," Uncle Jake said. "You still make those fantastic chocolate malteds?"

"You bet we do," Farrah said. "Sounds like you've been here before."

"A couple times." Uncle Jake sighed again.

"And what about you, honey?" Farrah said, turning to Sabrina. Waitresses in Manhattan were always calling her "honey." It made her a little homesick.

Sabrina read her order straight from the menu. "Cheeseburger, medium, cheese fries with a side of brown gravy, an egg cream, and . . ."

"What'cha lookin' for, darlin'?" Farrah asked.

"Oh, I wish you had blueberry cobbler. There was a diner near our apartment that specialized in it. Most restaurants don't make it."

"Well, we do." Farrah pointed to the bottom of the menu. Sabrina could have sworn it hadn't been there before but at the end of the dessert list was BLUEBERRY COBBLER in black and white.

"Looks like you've got the four major food groups covered," the waitress said with a playful wink. "How about you, short stuff?"

"I want chicken wings, some macaroni and cheese, and jalapeño poppers," Daphne said.

Farrah jotted it down.

"Then, for my main course, I would like one of these overstuffed Reuben sandwiches with extra Thousand Island dressing, a side of tater tots, a black-and-white milkshake, and a cherry vanilla Dr Pepper."

"Sweetie, there's no way you'll be able to eat all that." Farrah laughed.

"Oh, she'll eat it," Sabrina said. "Back home they call her 'The Stomach.'"

"Save me a slice of cheesecake, too," Daphne added after she'd stuck out her tongue at her sister.

Farrah laughed, shoved her pencil behind her ear, and dashed to the back with the order.

Suddenly, the door jingled and a crowd of people entered the diner. Leading them was the Queen of Hearts and Sheriff Nottingham. The queen called out a hello to everyone, while members of her entourage handed out "VOTE FOR HEART" buttons. The queen and the sheriff went from table to table, shaking hands with people and asking for votes. Sabrina frowned, knowing it was just a matter of time before they got to their table.

"Maybe we should leave," she said.

"Leave?" Daphne gasped. "Do you know how long it has been since I had chicken wings?"

"No, this will be fun," Uncle Jake said, just as Mrs. Heart and Nottingham reached their table. Without even looking, the queen took Uncle Jake's hand and shook it vigorously while her handlers pinned campaign buttons on the girls without bothering to ask if it was OK.

"Hello everyone, my name is Heart and I'm running for mayor of Ferryport Landing," the woman said.

"Hello, your majesty," Uncle Jake said with a mischievous grin.

The queen's eyes quickly darted to their uncle's face and immediately flared with rage.

"You!" she cried, yanking her hand away as if she had just put it inside a hornet's nest.

"Us," Daphne said.

"How is the campaign going?" Uncle Jake asked.

"It's going just fine, thank you." Mrs. Heart seethed. "Your assault on the community yesterday only helped get my point across. There's not enough room in this town for Everafters and Grimms."

"What an inspiring message of hope," Uncle Jake replied.

Sheriff Nottingham limped over and grabbed Jake by the collar. He pulled him close to his angry face and barked, "Laugh now, boy, but when we're running this town, I promise you I will personally squash your filthy vermin family under my boot heels."

"Take your hands off my uncle," Sabrina said.

Nottingham snarled. "Shut your gob, child, or I'll smack it off your face."

"What does *gob* mean?" Daphne asked.

Sabrina shrugged, reached into her pocket, took out the wand, and aimed it at the sheriff.

"Do you know what this is?" she asked.

Nottingham stared at the wand. "I don't have the foggiest," he growled.

"It's the Wand of Merlin," Sabrina said as she watched fear flash in Nottingham's eyes. Sabrina smiled, but inside she struggled with an overwhelming urge to zap the man with a shot of lightning.

"You're bluffing," Nottingham said.

"Is she?" Uncle Jake said.

Nottingham slowly let Jake go and stepped back from the table, but Sabrina kept pointing the wand at him. She had power for once and it felt good to let the bad guys know it.

Just then, there was an enormous thump that knocked the ketchup bottle off the table. It was followed by another, the source of which seemed to be outside. Everyone turned to look out at the parking lot where a car suddenly flipped over and went flying into another. A moment later a second car got the same destructive treatment.

Farrah returned with a tray of food and set the edge of it on the table. "Chow time!" she sang cheerily but her voice trailed off when she saw the destruction through the window. "Oh, my."

"What is that, Nottingham?" the queen demanded.

The would-be sheriff pointed out the window. "I think it's her."

Little Red Riding Hood came into view. She skipped through the parking lot like a happy schoolgirl, holding a leash, on the end of which walked her monstrous, reptilian playmate. The two demented creatures were coming straight for the diner.

"There's no cause for alarm," Nottingham said confidently just as the rest of the diners leaped from their seats and hid under the tables. An older gentleman jumped from his chair at the counter and knocked into Farrah, who spilled the family's meals all over the floor. The girls tumbled out of the booth and Sabrina's wand slipped from her hand and rolled to the other side of the room.

Nottingham opened his coat and pulled a serpentine sword from a scabbard strapped around his waist. He pointed it at the Jabberwocky but it made no impression on the beast. The hulking brute grabbed the front wall of the diner and tore it away as if it were paper. Then the creature poked its gruesome head into the hole, mere inches away from Sabrina and Daphne. It stuck out its long tongue and flicked it around as if it were tasting the fear in the room.

"JABBERWOCKY!" the monster cried.

7

Where's my grandmother?" Red Riding Hood screamed. Her face was a contorted mess, like a sculpture made from Silly Putty whose features were twisted and stretched into horrible exaggerations. "I want to play!"

"Stay down," Sabrina whispered to Daphne as Uncle Jake joined them on the floor.

Nottingham raised his sword and waved it in the air threateningly. "Child," he said to Red Riding Hood, "take this overgrown tadpole and go or I swear I'll—" but his threat was never finished. The Jabberwocky whipped its tail at him and sent him sailing across the room and into the dessert case. He let out a terrible groan and collapsed to the floor.

"Grandmother, are you in there?" the demented little girl called out, as she and the Jabberwocky stepped through the hole and into the diner. She searched with growing disappointment as patrons cowered under tables.

"Who are you looking for, young lady?" the queen called out with a trembling voice.

"My grandmother," Red Riding Hood said. Her face suddenly went from rage to a sweet hopeful smile.

The Queen of Hearts smiled, too, or at least did something Sabrina guessed was as close as the nasty woman could get to smiling. "But child, your grandmother is dead. Don't you remember? She was eaten by the Big Bad Wolf."

Red Riding Hood sputtered and rocked back and forth on her feet. "That's not true," she said to herself, over and over again. "We're playing a game. I have to find her so my family can be together again. She's just hiding. Playing a game."

"Oh, you poor thing," the queen said. "You're so confused."

"That's what they said," the little girl agreed as her face darkened. "I'm confused. They said I had . . . imagination."

The Jabberwocky leaned down to the little girl and licked her face with his long disgusting tongue, causing her to giggle. "Oh, kitty, are you bored? Do you want to play? I bet this lady would like to play with you."

The Jabberwocky gnashed its teeth enthusiastically and turned to Mrs. Heart. It reached over and snatched her off the ground in one of its huge, taloned hands. She screamed and begged for help.

"Do something!" Sabrina whispered to her uncle. She didn't like the Queen of Hearts, not even a little, but she didn't want her to die, either.

Uncle Jake rolled his eyes and sighed. "Fine," he grumbled. He sprang to his feet and pointed a threatening finger at the brute. "Hey, ugly—put her down!"

"You know where my grandmother is! You know where the doggy is, too. Don't you?" Red Riding Hood said.

"Yes, yes!" the queen cried as struggled to free herself. "He's the one you want! Not me! There's no need to kill me!"

The Jabberwocky gnashed its fangs and dropped the Queen of Hearts. It stomped across the room toward the Grimms, tossing tables and chairs out of its way

"Uncle Jake? It's coming," Sabrina cried impatiently.

"Working on it, kid," Uncle Jake said. He searched his many pockets for something that he could use against the monster. Pennies, buttons, half a candy bar, and dozens of trinkets and necklaces were tossed aside. "I have just the thing in here. Where on earth did I put it?" But whatever he was searching for he didn't find. The monster backhanded him so hard he crashed through the men's room door.

The Jabberwocky beat on its chest and flapped its leathery wings. It shrieked and spit and then chaos ensued. The monster stomped its colossal foot down on the floor, causing a shock-wave that rolled through the diner. Chairs flew through the ceiling and walls, and exploded into the dessert case right above the still-unconscious Nottingham. Several cups of butterscotch pudding tipped over and dribbled down onto his head.

Sabrina scrambled across the room toward her wand. Just as she snatched it, the Jabberwocky leaped forward and set a heavy paw on Sabrina's chest, pinning her arms at her side. She couldn't move an inch. The monster craned its neck so that its nose was touching Sabrina's and it sprayed its hot, pungent breath into her face.

"I want my grandmother and my doggy," Red Riding Hood said as she crossed the room and stood over Sabrina. "And I want them right now."

"You're crazy!" Sabrina cried. "Your family is dead!"

"You're making me mad and you're making kitty mad, too!"

The Jabberwocky growled and gnashed its teeth.

"Fine! I give up," a voice said. Sabrina recognized the voice as Puck's but couldn't see its owner. She heard a whizzing sound above her. It infuriated the Jabberwocky, which turned to face the boy, freeing Sabrina. She crawled back to her hiding sister and together they got to their feet. There was Puck, hovering in the hole in the diner, with his beautiful pink-streaked wings flapping in the sun. He held a slingshot that was loaded with a broken brick from the diner's crumbling wall. He loaded the slingshot, pulled the brick back, and let it fly. It smacked into one of the Jabberwocky's eyes and the beast shrieked. "You've beaten me, Grimms. Are you happy? You dragged me into this hero business against my will and now every time I turn around, I'm saving the day. Well, I hope you're happy. I'm a hero now."

Red Riding Hood screamed. "I don't want to play this game!"

"Hey, let's play the quiet game," Puck shouted at the little girl. "Your crazy talk is distracting from my heroics. If I'm going to be a good guy, then people are going to notice."

Instantly, the Jabberwocky lunged at Puck, using its long claws to knock the boy out of the sky. Puck fell hard to the ground, unable to defend himself as the monster reached down and grabbed hold of him with one hand. It lifted Puck up to its face and examined him closely.

"Don't worry, girls," Puck shouted, almost laughing. "I've got all this under control!"

With one lightning-fast motion, the Jabberwocky reached over, grabbed hold of Puck's magical pink fairy wings, and ripped them off his back. The sound was excruciating.

"Puck!" the girls shouted.

The fairy boy cried out in agony and the Jabberwocky tossed him hard against a wall. He didn't get up again.

Sabrina gazed around the room, feeling as if the world were in slow motion. She had a terrifying sense of helplessness, the way she felt in so many of her recent nightmares, and she was tired of it. She squeezed the wand in her hand, and aimed it at the monster. Storm clouds suddenly filled the air. Lightning crackled and a bolt shot out of the sky and hit the Jabberwocky in the chest. There was an enormous explosion and the monster fell onto its back. A smoldering black burn remained where the lightning had struck the beast.

An electrifying sensation raced through Sabrina. She felt like she had plugged into a light socket and replaced her blood with its current. She could have sworn at that moment that her eyes were on fire and she was a hundred feet tall. The amount of raw energy she had at her disposal was incredible. She was shocked when the Jabberwocky stirred and crawled to its feet.

"You want some more? Fine!" she shouted. Another lightning

blast caught the monster on the top of its head. It fell to the ground again. This time Sabrina took a step closer, only to have the beast's head curl toward her. She was nearly bitten. Now, she was shaking, not from fear, but anger at the monster's defiance of her power. *How dare this thing continue to live!*

She shook the wand angrily and summoned another crash of lightning, and another, and another until her ears rang from the deafening thunder that came with every bolt. "Stay down!" she shouted, unable to hear her own words, but the monster refused. It got up, again and again and again, and each time it took a step closer to her and her little sister.

Finally, the smoking hulk had backed them into a corner. Covered in wounds and burns, it shrieked into Sabrina's face. She turned to her sister and slipped her hand into Daphne's.

Just then, much to Sabrina's disbelief, the Jabberwocky was lifted off its feet and slammed to the ground. The impact sent the girls tumbling over each other.

"I didn't do that," Sabrina said, staring down at the wand she still clutched in her hand.

"Doggy!" Red Riding Hood shouted, and clapped.

Sabrina turned to see what the little girl was raving about. There, standing over the monster, was an unusual man. He was excruciatingly thin, and wearing a suit that was several sizes too big for him. He had watery eyes and feeble hands. He also had a shock of white, unruly hair.

"Mr. . . . Canis?" Sabrina stammered.

"Mr. Canis!" Daphne cried, leaping up to race into his arms. Sabrina stared at their old friend, then grabbed her sister and pulled her back down. There was something different about him. He had bright blue eyes—the same color as those of his alter ego, the Big Bad Wolf.

The Jabberwocky didn't stay down long. It fought its way to its feet and tore into the old man, pounding its huge paws into Mr. Canis's chest. Despite the horrific blows, Mr. Canis seemed more than capable of handling the monster's abuse and dishing out some of his own. One swing from his elderly fist sent the Jabberwocky sailing through the hole in the diner's wall and into the parking lot. Cars went flying and pavement crumbled under its skidding body.

"Look! The doggy and the kitty are going to be friends," Red Riding Hood shouted.

Sabrina got to her feet and pointed the wand at the deranged little girl.

"Where are my parents, you little psychopath?" she cried. The little girl snarled like a wild animal and lunged to scratch Sabrina across the face.

"They're *my* parents!" she raged.

"You tell me right now or I'm going to fry you," Sabrina threatened, deflecting the little girl's attack and pointing the wand in her face. She could sense the clouds forming in the sky again. All she had to do was think it and the little girl would be a stain on the floor.

"I'm going to have my grandmother!" the little girl screamed in anger.

The air around Sabrina began to crack and pop. She knew she was about to unleash the lightning on the little girl and felt she had a right to do it. "You're asking for it!"

Suddenly, the wand was knocked out of Sabrina's hand. She turned and saw Daphne standing next to her.

"Sabrina, no!"

"Tell my grandmother I'm coming," Red Riding Hood shouted. She lifted her hand and the ring on her finger cast a crimson light on the room. A moment later, both she and the Jabberwocky disappeared into thin air.

"How could you, Daphne? She's got Mom and Dad!"

"Puck needs our help," Daphne shouted.

The two girls rushed to the fallen fairy's side, but Mr. Canis was already lifting him into his arms. "Get home, children," he said roughly as he dashed away at an amazing speed. Sabrina had never seen anyone, man or Everafter, run so fast. Before the girls knew it, Canis and Puck were gone.

"Uncle Jake," Daphne said, turning and racing to find their uncle. When they did, he was still unconscious. Their waitress, Farrah, was standing over him.

"Don't worry, girls. I don't think he's too hurt," she said. She tossed a glass of water into Jake's face and he quickly opened his eyes. "We get a lot of drunks in here around two a.m. This works every time."

Uncle Jake shook his head and looked around. "What did I miss?"

"Let's just put it this way," Farrah said. "It's going to be a little while on the blueberry cobbler."

• • •

After Glinda the Good Witch scattered forgetful dust on the bewildered human diner customers and Sheriff Hamstead checked to make sure everyone was OK, the family got a high-speed police escort back home.

"Granny!" Sabrina shouted as they ran into the house. The old woman called to them from upstairs and the girls raced to find her. They burst into the old woman's bedroom and found her sitting next to Puck, who was in her bed covered in blankets. Both the girls tried to explain everything that had happened at the same time.

"*Lieblings*, it's OK!" Granny shouted over them. The girls stopped talking and struggled to catch their breaths.

"Mr. Canis is alive," Daphne said.

"Of course I am," a voice said from the corner. They turned and found an exhausted-looking Mr. Canis sitting in a chair. The old man had never been the picture of health, but now he looked especially bad. His eyes were bloodshot and his face seemed to be hanging onto his head for dear life.

"It's happening again?" Hamstead said when he stepped into the room and saw the old man.

"No, it is different this time," Mr. Canis said as his blue eyes flashed in the dark room. He pulled himself to his feet and leaned against the wall. "The explosion changed some things in unexpected ways. I have access to the Wolf's abilities but my control over him is . . . fading. I am also having some difficulties completing the change to my human form."

He turned slightly to show the bushy brown tail sticking out the back of his trousers.

Sabrina turned to her grandmother. "Did you know he was still alive?"

Granny Relda nodded. "Yes."

"You lied to us!"

"Because I asked her to," Canis said. "I wanted to save you from having to mourn my death twice."

"I don't understand," Daphne said.

"He means he was going to kill himself," Sabrina said. "Why?"

"Because I would rather die than let the Wolf loose again. Every one of his victims lives inside my mind. I hear them beg for mercy that never came. I see the terror in their faces as they died. I will never let him free again. His crimes are *still* destroying lives, including your own. You've seen today the repercussions of his violence."

"You drove Little Red Riding Hood insane," Sabrina said.

"I took her family from her," Mr. Canis whispered. The old man hung his tired head.

Sheriff Hamstead turned to the girls. "Red Riding Hood has never been the same. When the Everafters from Europe came over on Wilhelm's ship, she spent the entire voyage raving to herself, drawing these horrible pictures, and screaming through the night. Even the ogres were terrified of her. When we all got settled in Ferryport Landing, our first order of business was finding a place to keep her. We built the asylum at the top of Mount Taurus, hired a few Everafter doctors and nurses to look after her, and basically forgot about her. But she kept finding ways to escape, so something had to be done."

"Spaulding Grimm went to Baba Yaga and asked her to cast the same spell on the asylum that she'd used to trap everyone in the town," Granny Relda said. "It was a brilliant idea. Anyone who became a serious problem got sent to the asylum."

"That's where we put the Jabberwocky, as well," Sheriff Hamstead added.

"But the spell that keeps everyone in the town is big-time magic. How did Red Riding Hood get loose again?" Sabrina asked.

Granny Relda turned to Uncle Jake. He seemed to sink into his clothing.

"Tell them, Mom. Tell them everything," he said.

Granny's face looked pained but she took a few deep breaths and stood up from her chair. She turned to a framed photo on the wall. It was of her and their grandpa Basil when the two were much younger. Sabrina guessed they were in their mid-twenties. Even though the photo was in black and white, it couldn't hide the color in their faces. Their eyes and cheeks glowed. They were young and in love. Granny took the photo off the wall and looked at it lovingly.

"Oh, where to start? I guess at the beginning. When I was twenty-six I met a man at a party in Berlin. A week later I married him. His name was Basil Grimm.

"I didn't know anything about the Grimm family really, other than what I had learned about Jacob and Wilhelm in school. All I knew was that Basil was a handsome, adventurous, slightly arrogant American who swept me off my feet. He told me we were going on vacation. It would be the last vacation we ever took, but we packed memories into it that would last a lifetime. We traveled the globe together on a two-year honeymoon.

"We went everywhere: Istanbul, Hawaii, Alaska, the Amazon, South Africa, the Galápagos Islands—it was exhilarating. Every morning we woke up in a strange new land, hungry to explore. These were some of the happiest times of my life. A year into the trip I got pregnant with your father, but it didn't stop our adventure. We continued to travel even after he was born."

Granny put the photo back and crossed the room to where another framed photo hung. This one was of the couple in a snowy landscape, running a dogsled. She took it off the wall and admired it.

"Before the two years were quite up, Basil got a letter from his sister Matilda telling him he had to come home. His brother, your great-uncle Edwin, had passed away, so we came to Ferryport Landing as quickly as we could. And then I was introduced to the family business."

Granny put the photo back on the wall.

"Your Uncle Jake was born a year later, shortly after Matilda passed away from pneumonia. Basil was proud of his boys and was determined that they would carry on the family responsibility. Even when they were babies, he would stand over their cribs and read them fairy tales. When they were five, he set them loose in the Hall of Wonders, giving them free rein and sets of keys of their own. When other boys their age were playing baseball, Henry and Jacob were playing with magic wands and flying carpets and dragons. By the time they were young men, they were as apt at magical weaponry and lore as any Everafter in the town."

Uncle Jake cleared his throat. "I'll take it from here, Mom. When your father turned twenty, he was in love with someone. This was before he met your mother," he explained. "She was an Everafter and it broke his heart to know she was trapped in this town. It broke my heart to see him so sad, especially on his birthday. I wanted to give him something special. So I turned off the barrier so she could escape."

Everyone gasped, especially Sheriff Hamstead. "How?" he squealed.

"I snuck into Baba Yaga's house and found her spell book. The spell I discovered was simple, and it would only shut the barrier down for a moment. It was all I needed. Hank's girlfriend waited for the spell to take effect and then she stepped through. We both couldn't wait to see Hank's face when he saw her waving to him from the other side. We had no idea what we had done.

"Dropping the barrier also dropped a few other similar barrier spells, including the one Baba Yaga had put on the asylum," Uncle Jake explained. "Anyone who had been put in there for the good of the town was freed, including Red Riding Hood and the Jabberwocky.

"Well, when I discovered what had happened, I went after the monster," Uncle Jake said. "I chased it through the forest without even thinking about what I would do if I caught up to it, but I never got a chance to come up with a plan. It found me and I was cornered on a cliff."

"I know the cliff," Sabrina said, realizing that she and her uncle had faced the monster at the same spot.

"And Grandpa came to save you," Daphne said.

"He was a hero who loved his sons," Granny Relda said softly.

"He never came home, again," Uncle Jake said. "They took

him to the hospital and he died a day later. The monster disappeared into the woods along with Red Riding Hood, and they've been missing ever since."

Sabrina looked into her uncle's face and saw an old heartbreak.

"Your father needed some time to himself, so he left for New York City the day after the funeral," Granny Relda said. "He met your mother shortly after and they fell in love. They moved back here for a year, and Veronica was inducted into the family business just like I was, but each mystery they uncovered unnerved your father more and more. He worried something would happen to his new bride and when she announced she was pregnant with you, Sabrina, they left town. Your father vowed to me that his children would have nothing to do with magic, Everafters, or the Hall of Wonders."

"I left town after the funeral, too, and haven't been back until yesterday," Jake said. "I couldn't let that thing hurt another person because of something I did."

"Why don't I remember any of this happening?" Sheriff Hamstead asked, suspiciously.

"I'm sorry, Ernest. I had to make you all forget. When news spread that a Grimm knew how to drop the barrier, things got very ugly. People were getting hurt and I had to find a way to stop it."

"I've always wondered how I'd react if I knew I could break the spell. I hope I was a gentleman," Hamstead said.

Granny smiled. "You were one of my heroes."

The sheriff nodded. "I suppose I can't be angry. I've scattered a lot of forgetful dust myself. Any other big secrets, Relda?"

The old woman grinned uncomfortably.

"Never mind," the sheriff said.

Sabrina looked down at Puck. He was fevered, pale, and unconscious. "What can we do for him?" she asked.

"He's hurt . . . badly," Granny replied.

"We can't let him die," Daphne said as tears spilled onto her cheeks.

"We should search the Hall of Wonders for something that will heal him," Sabrina said.

Granny pointed to a collection of empty tins, tubes, and bottles on the nightstand.

"Then we'll try something else," Sabrina argued.

"And we will fail, child," Mr. Canis said. "He's not like you. He's not even like most of the Everafters, creatures touched by magic. He's a creature *of* magic."

"Then what? We just give up? We have to do something!"

"He needs to be with his own people. He needs to be in Faerie," the old man said. "They will know how to help him."

"Let's go!" Daphne cried.

"We can't," Granny said.

"The barrier," Sabrina whispered as she lowered her eyes. Puck was lying there in front of her, probably dying, all because of some stupid two-hundred-year-old spell.

"Wait, you said you knew how to turn off the barrier," Hamstead said to Uncle Jake.

"Absolutely not," Granny Relda said before her son could answer. "Red Riding Hood and the Jabberwocky escaped from the asylum when the barrier fell the first time. We can't risk them escaping the town, too."

"I have an idea that could solve all our problems," Uncle Jake said.

Everyone turned to him and listened.

"The Vorpal blade," Uncle Jake replied.

"You mean that thing Mr. van Winkle mentioned the other day?" Daphne asked.

"Lewis Caroll wrote about it in *Alice's Adventures in Wonderland.* It's a magical sword and supposedly the only thing that can kill a Jabberwocky."

"He's right," Sabrina added. "I read about it in the family

journals. It not only killed the other Jabberwockies, but it also cut a hole in the barrier. The Black Knight used it to escape Ferryport Landing."

"So you see," Uncle Jake said. "We could use it to kill the Jabberwocky, rescue Hank and Veronica, and cut a hole into the barrier big enough to get Puck out so we can take him to the Faerie folk."

"Well, what are we waiting for?" Daphne cried.

Granny Relda lowered her eyes. "Spaulding Grimm had the Vorpal blade destroyed. After he trapped the Jabberwocky in the asylum and had Baba Yaga cast the spell, he figured the sword was too dangerous to keep around. Someone could have used it to escape town. He had it broken into three pieces and scattered them. I don't know who has the pieces..."

Sabrina's heart sank. Puck would certainly die now.

"Except for one," Granny finished. She opened a drawer in her nightstand and took out a swatch of green velvet. Inside was something long and heavy. She placed it into Uncle Jake's hands.

Uncle Jake unwrapped the object. It was metal and shiny. He lifted it to reveal the hilt of a sword. Only a small jagged portion of the steel remained. An inscription was carved into the metal.

"What are we going to do with a broken sword?" Daphne said.

"I don't know," Granny replied. "But maybe we can find the other pieces. I believe the inscription is a clue Spaulding left for us in case we ever needed the sword again."

Uncle Jake read it. "'Find the daughter of the water.' Who is the daughter of the water?"

"Even if we find this daughter of the water and get the other pieces, is there someone in this town who can put the sword back together?" Hamstead interjected.

"The Vorpal blade was supposed to be indestructible," Uncle Jake said. "Spaulding needed to find someone with some seriously powerful mojo to break it. There's only one person in this town who can do something like that."

"The Blue Fairy," Canis said.

"From the Pinocchio story?" Sabrina asked.

"The same. The Blue Fairy is like a nuclear reactor of magic. She can grant any wish. She turned a wooden doll into a real boy. Even Baba Yaga doesn't have power over life and death."

"So, problem solved. We'll find the other pieces and take them to the Blue Fairy," Sabrina said.

"No one knows who the Blue Fairy is," Granny Relda said. "I

know she lives in town, but the spell she uses to disguise herself is powerful. I suppose I would want my privacy, too, if I could grant wishes and bring things to life. People would always want to take advantage of a power like that."

"Then what's the point of all this?" Daphne cried. "Even if we find the pieces, we can't put them together. We can't kill the Jabberwocky or get Puck to the Faerie folk."

"Have faith, *liebling*," Granny said, wrapping her arms around the little girl's shoulders. "If Spaulding left us clues for finding the pieces, I'm sure he gave us a clue for finding the Blue Fairy so she can put them back together."

"I'll return to the forest and continue to track the girl and the monster," Mr. Canis said as he stood up weakly.

"I've got to get a handle on what happened at the diner," Hamstead said. "If too many humans drive by and see the destruction, I'll have to dust the town again. Good luck with your search."

The Sheriff and Canis left the room.

Granny sat down on the bed and took both of the girls' hands in her own. "I've tried to keep you away from this for as long as I can." The old woman sighed. "I thought if we hid from all of it maybe it would go away. Sabrina, I know you thought I didn't care but I did. I lost my husband, my son, my daughter-in-law, and thought I would never see Jacob again. I couldn't stand to lose the two of you. I didn't want to put you in danger."

"Don't worry, Granny," Daphne said as she hugged the old woman.

"We are Grimms. This is what we do," Sabrina added as she hugged the old woman.

"We should get started on research, girls," Uncle Jake said. "I'm sure if we dig into the journals, we'll find some reference to this 'daughter of the water.' "

"Maybe it's a fish," Daphne said.

"I've had that sword for decades and I've had a lot of time to think about what Spaulding meant. I don't think it's a fish, but I think you're close," Granny Relda said. She cupped her hand around Daphne's ear and whispered something that made the girl's eyes grow as big as Frisbees.

"No way!" Daphne cried as she inserted her palm into her mouth and bit down hard.

• • •

The sun was near the end of its decline by the time the girls and their uncle rowed out to the middle of the Hudson River in a tiny boat. Uncle Jake had been tight-lipped about his plan. When he reached the spot he was looking for, he dropped a bright orange anchor overboard.

"The Little Mermaid is the seventh daughter of Poseidon, the ruler of the sea," he said as he fumbled in his pockets. Eventually he took out a small fishing rod. On it was a lure and a hook.

"What kind of magic is that?" Daphne asked.

"It's not magic. It's called a Pocket Fisherman. I bought it on the Internet," Uncle Jake cast his line. "Spaulding knew what he was doing. Giving the blade to the Little Mermaid was a great way to hide it."

Every time they mentioned the Little Mermaid's name, Daphne jumped up in excitement, nearly capsizing the boat several times. She had seen a movie about the character at a friend's house when she was five and spent entire weekends in the bathtub trying to grow fins. Of all the Everafters in the town, Daphne wanted to meet the undersea princess the most.

"I bet we'll become best friends," Daphne said. "She'll invite me over all the time."

"Sure, who wouldn't want to spend all their free time at the bottom of the Hudson River?" Sabrina said. "Did you ever think that all of this is a wild-goose chase? We can't exactly breathe underwater."

"Don't worry, 'Brina," Uncle Jake said as he reeled in his line's slack. "I know someone who can help us with that."

It was several minutes before Sabrina noticed a tugging on the line.

"Looks like I've got a bite," Uncle Jake said, slowly and cautiously reeling his catch in. Suddenly, he pulled back hard on the rod, and from the tension in it, it seemed as if he had hooked a big one. The fish was strong. A few times Sabrina was sure the fishing rod would be ripped out of Uncle Jake's hands and dragged underwater, but her uncle was strong and soon he was pulling thc fish onboard.

It was huge, probably weighing twenty pounds, with a white belly, gray skin, and a series of purple stripes on either side of its back. It flopped around on the bottom of the boat, smacking against the girls with its tail, and then it did something so shocking Sabrina nearly fell overboard.

"Jake Grimm!" the fish said in a gurgling voice. "You dirty, filthy, no good, pain in my fin! I should have known when I saw that lure that it was either you or your lousy brother!"

"How are you doing, Anthony?" Uncle Jake said as he set his rod into the boat. "I wish this could have been avoided, bud, but we need a bit of your special talents."

"You're a talking fish," Daphne said.

"And you're a master of the obvious," Anthony said. "Are these your kids, Jake? If this brood is the future of the Grimms, I suspect your family is in deep trouble. So, what do you want?"

"We're going to see the Little Mermaid and we need to be able to breathe underwater," Uncle Jake explained.

"Not a good idea!" the fish warned.

"It can't be avoided," Uncle Jake replied. "The mermaid's got something we need."

"She's in a foul mood lately. She's been particularly abusive to her staff. Half of them have been turned into fish sticks. If she kills you, don't come crying to me. I tried to warn you."

"Kills us?" Daphne cried. "That's crazy talk! The Little Mermaid would never kill someone. I know, I saw the movie!"

"She's mean!" Anthony said as he flopped around the boat. "Mean, I tell you!"

"Shut your mouth," Daphne cried. "I don't believe a word you say."

"Your funeral," the fish gurgled. "All right, Jake. You know how this works. Make your wish."

"Wait a minute. You grant wishes?" Sabrina interrupted.

"I'm a fish that talks and you're having trouble with me granting wishes?"

"Why are we wishing to be able to breathe underwater? Why don't we just wish we had all the pieces of the Vorpal blade? Why not avoid the headache!" Sabrina asked her uncle.

"Sorry kid, one wish per customer. I can't grant multipart wishes," the fish said.

"Well, then I wish I had the Little Mermaid's part of the Vorpal blade," Sabrina said.

Just then, a seaweed-covered piece of metal materialized in Sabrina's hands. She picked off the slimy plants and smiled. Its jagged end would fit perfectly with the other piece of the sword.

"All right, Jake," the fish said. "I did my part. Now put me back in the water."

"I really appreciate your help," Uncle Jake said as he scooped the fish up and released him into the river. Anthony drifted back up to the surface and squirted water into Uncle Jake's face.

"Next time, put a worm on that hook. If I'm going to be put out, the least you could do is feed me!"

The fish dove under the waves and was gone while the family eyed their treasure with awe.

"That was easy enough," Sabrina said.

"Magic makes everything easier," Uncle Jake said.

Daphne shrugged. "Granny says there is always a price for using magic."

"Your grandmother just likes to do things the hard way," Uncle Jake said.

Suddenly, there was mighty splash and a figure sprang out of the water. He was strong, with a barrel chest and big arms. His skin was green-tinged and he had kelp in his hair. He yanked an orange starfish from a belt around his waist and smacked it onto the top of Daphne's head. He snatched her in his arms and dragged her under the water.

"Daphne!" Sabrina cried as she searched the surface for her sister.

Sabrina and Uncle Jake desperately called out for the little girl, but there was no reply. Had her sister just been drowned before her eyes? Seconds later there was another splash on the other side of the boat. This time, Sabrina got a better look at what kind of man it was. She noticed, to her shock, that he had a fish tail instead of legs. He slapped another starfish onto Uncle Jake's head and before Sabrina could put up a fight, her uncle was dragged overboard as well.

Sabrina was all alone. She stuffed the sword piece into one coat pocket and out of another she took the Wand of Merlin. She studied the water, examining every ripple and preparing for an attack. When she heard the splash behind her, she spun around, causing the little boat to dip and roll. She lost her balance and the wand fell from her hand and rolled to the bottom of the boat. Before Sabrina could scamper down to retrieve it, the merman sprang into the boat, nearly capsizing it. He removed a scroll from a little bag on his belt and unfurled it, then cleared his throat and began to read.

"By the order or our lady, the princess, I do hereby place you and your co-conspirators under arrest for acts of thievery," the merman declared.

"You don't understand!" Sabrina argued, but the merman ignored her. He rolled up his scroll and tucked it back into his bag. Then he slapped an orange starfish onto the top of Sabrina's head. The starfish's five arms clamped down on her skull, acting like suction cups, and suddenly an odd sensation came over her. She literally felt like a fish out of water. She couldn't breathe!

8

What have you done to me?” Sabrina gasped, desperate for air.

“Silence, you filthy, thieving topsider!” the merman barked as he snatched the piece of the Vorpal blade from her pocket. He tucked it under his belt and then grabbed her roughly by the arm. Before Sabrina could struggle, he leaped out of the boat and into the frigid water, taking her with him.

He swam deeper and deeper with Sabrina trapped in his strong grasp. She fought back viciously, punching and kicking her captor, but it didn't seem to faze the merman at all. Soon, her lungs were burning for oxygen. Her mouth instinctively opened and she inhaled deeply. Icy crystals raced down her throat. A curious heaviness filled her body and she felt as if water were pouring into her fingers and toes. She closed her eyes, preparing to die, but after several minutes something dawned on her—she could breathe! *It must be the starfish,* she realized.

"Where are you taking me?" Sabrina demanded as a wave of bubbles escaped her mouth. She was surprised to find her voice sounded as normal as it did in air.

The merman said nothing, only pointed to the rapidly approaching river floor where an incredible sight came into view. Nestled on the rocky bottom of the Hudson River was a city. It had skyscrapers, apartment buildings, and hundreds of mermen and mermaids rushing here and there in the neatly planned grid of streets. From high above, the city was a fantastically beautiful dream of green and aquamarine, but as the merman dragged her closer and closer, the city's secret began to reveal itself. Everything was made out of trash. Entire buildings were made from discarded car tires and license plates. The sidewalks were paved with old bottle caps and the heels of shoes. Homes were constructed from old clothes, wagon wheels, flip-flops, garden tools, computers, antique telephones, grocery carts, beach chairs, cans, bottles, and thousands of tennis balls, footballs, and Frisbees, all stacked with expert care.

The merman pulled Sabrina through the city gates and along a street made of crushed toasters and cast-iron skillets.

"Where did you get all this stuff?" Sabrina said.

The merman scowled and pointed toward the surface. She looked up, then down again at all the junk. No wonder her captor had so much contempt for her. Every nook and cranny of the odd city owed its existence to two hundred years of junk that people like herself had dumped into the river. Human beings were disgusting.

He turned down one alley and then another. They passed dozens of shops carved out of sunken sailboats—some still had their names painted on the side. Merman and mermaid shop owners stood on the street calling out to passersby, trying to get them to buy old pop bottles and bicycle wheels. A mermother pushed an infant merbaby along the street in an old stroller.

Soon Sabrina and the merman reached an enormous palace, nearly five stories high. From above, Sabrina had thought it was the most beautiful place she had ever seen, but now that she was in front of it she realized it was made of the same junk as the rest of the underwater town. A flight of stairs, which were actually old car bumpers, led to a large door which was guarded by a merman holding a dented trumpet in one hand and a trident in the other.

"I have the last of the topsider prisoners," her captor said.

The merman guard nodded. "You may pass." He swam over

and pushed the door open, allowing them to enter a great seaweed-covered hallway. They continued through another doorway, this one unguarded, and down a flight of steps. At the bottom Sabrina saw several heavy wooden doors with metal bars on their windows. The merman took a set of keys from his belt, opened up the closest door, and shoved Sabrina inside. Daphne and Uncle Jake sat on a bench in the corner of the room. Daphne looked at her disapprovingly, while Uncle Jake gave her a pitiful smile.

"You will be held here in the dungeon until her highness seeks your presence," the merman barked. "Then you will be given five minutes to plead your innocence or guilt. Shortly after, you will be executed and your bodies fed to the lake's parasites and bottom-feeders."

"What if we're found innocent?" Sabrina said.

"No one is found innocent," the merman said. He exited the room, slammed the heavy metal door, and locked it tight.

Sabrina turned back to her family. "I dropped the wand into the boat."

"It doesn't matter anyway," Uncle Jake said. "It won't work underwater."

"If I am fed to bottom-feeders, I will never forgive you!" Daphne said. "You *had* to use magic. Granny said there was always a price, but you wouldn't listen. What are we going to do now?"

"I don't know. We're in big trouble," Uncle Jake said.

Sabrina and Daphne looked at each other. They didn't have to say what they were thinking. In the short time they had known their uncle, he had been Mr. Confidence. If he was giving up already, then the situation was really bad.

"You don't know?" Sabrina said. "You've got an overcoat filled with magic stuff. Start searching your pockets."

"I doubt anything will work. Magic doesn't like getting wet," Uncle Jake said.

"We don't need any of your magic," Daphne said. "I'll do all the talking. I'll tell the princess why we need her part of the sword. She's the Little Mermaid. She's really cool and nice and she'll totally understand."

"Daphne, this isn't the Little Mermaid from the movies," Uncle Jake explained. "In that movie she fell in love with the prince and was happy, but in the real story, the one Hans Christian Andersen documented, the princess gave up her entire life to be with her prince and he abandoned her for another woman. He rode off and completely forgot about her. She's never really gotten over it, and is still a little resentful toward humans. Actually, that's an understatement. She hates humans, especially men. Hell hath no fury like a woman scorned."

"What does *scorned* mean?" Daphne asked her sister.

"It means she got dumped," Sabrina answered, then turned her attention back to her uncle. "So what are we going to do?"

Just then, the door flew open and two hulking merman guards entered. They wore heavy steel helmets and carried silver tridents, which they pointed at the group.

"The princess will see you now," one of them shouted as he swam over and grabbed Jake. The second brute clamped his big hands on the two girls and dragged them out of the cell. The guards forced the family down the hallway, and into a massive, high-ceilinged room and up to a pair of enormous doors covered in seaweed. An elderly merman with a bushy white beard and spectacles stood nearby at a podium reading a soggy book.

"Yes?" the old merman said without looking up.

"I have the topsiders who stole from the princess," one of the guards said respectfully.

The old merman took off his glasses and squinted as he examined the group. "Yes, yes, let them in," he shouted. Instantly a school of catfish swam up to the door. Each grabbed on to a strand of seaweed with its mouth and together they swung the mighty doors open.

The room on the other side was expansive, and though constructed out of trash, everything gleamed as if it were made from marble. In the center of the room was the backseat of an old car. It was strung with brilliant white pearls and sat on a pedestal of discarded milk crates. Sabrina thought it resembled a throne but it hardly seemed regal.

The merman guards escorted the girls and their uncle up to the pedestal and forced them onto their knees.

"Show some respect, ground-walkers!" one of the guards barked.

Just then, a door on the far side of the chamber opened and several mermen swam into the room, carrying dented and broken musical instruments. They blew some bubbly, off-key notes, then a tall, thin merman holding a stone tablet swam forward. "All hail, Poseidon's princess. Her majesty, the Little Mermaid!"

Sabrina craned her neck to see the princess, but just then an outrageously overweight mermaid swam through the doors and blocked her view. It wasn't until two mermen helped the enormous half-woman/half-fish onto the throne that Sabrina realized she was indeed looking at the legendary Little Mermaid. It took her assistants several minutes to get the princess into her seat and then several minutes more for the mermaid to get comfortable.

When she was done, she was wheezing like a teakettle. Still, her overabundant body couldn't hide the beauty she was. She had big blue eyes and a mane of gorgeous red hair that flowed to her ankles. She wore a seashell bikini top and an aquamarine sarong. On her head was a pearl-encrusted tiara.

"That's the *Little* Mermaid?" Sabrina said quietly to Uncle Jake.

Uncle Jake nodded. "The breakup was very hard on her. She turned to food for comfort."

The princess picked up a conch shell sitting on the armrest of her throne and blew into it. A low rumbling note filled the air.

"I am hungry. I want a treat," she demanded.

The skinny merman with the tablet approached the throne. "Your highness, if you will recall, last week you instructed me to not allow you to snack between meals. You told me to kill anyone who offers you anything that isn't on your diet."

"I'm rescinding that order," the princess said. "I want a treat. I've been good all day. I had my seaweed smoothie for breakfast and lunch and I swam on the treadmill for twenty minutes. I want a treat. I deserve a treat."

"But, your majesty . . ."

"Treat!" she roared. *"Now!"*

"Very well, your highness," the merman said with a worried face. "Bring the princess a treat!"

A second merman soldier shouted, "Bring the princess a treat!" followed by another and another. Soon, the side door flew open and a lowly merman wearing a chef's hat and a white apron swam into the hall with a dented silver platter. He bowed before the princess, took the lid off, and presented a bright pink cake with squiggly tentacles poking out of the sides. She snatched it from him with greedy fingers.

"It's anemone upside-down cake, your majesty," the chef said nervously. He bowed deeply, left the platter, and hurried off. The princess took a big bite of the odd cake. Sabrina knew her grandmother would die to have the recipe.

"Oh, it's heavenly," the little mermaid said with her mouth full. "I think I'll have another tiny bite."

She ate another, and then another, and another until the whole cake was gone. She looked down at the empty platter and started to cry.

"My lady," the skinny merman said nervously. "What brings you to tears?"

"I'm fat!" she cried. "Look at me! I used to be thin! How could you let me eat that cake?"

"But, your majesty . . ."

"It's the chef's fault. I want you to feed him to the Cruel Crustacean!"

"But, your majesty. He's your favorite chef."

"Cruel Crustacean!" she roared. *"Now!"*

"Feed the chef to the Cruel Crustacean!" the merman assistant shouted. It was quickly repeated throughout the room until a hulking guard ran out the side door with his trident.

"What's the Cruel Crustacean?" Daphne whispered.

Sabrina shrugged. "Uncle Jake, do something."

"What?"

"I don't know. You said you were good with women. You figure it out," Sabrina said.

Uncle Jake smiled. "Your majesty, I think you're being too hard on yourself. I don't think you're fat. I think you're beautiful."

One of the merman guards stuck his trident dangerously close to Uncle Jake's throat. *"Silence!"* he shouted. "You will not speak until the princess has given you permission."

"Who are these topsiders?" the mermaid asked as she licked the crumbs off her fingers.

"These are the ones who stole your portion of the Vorpal blade," the skinny merman explained to the princess. He set the broken sword on the throne and then backed away.

"Is this true, topsider? Defend yourself!" the Little Mermaid demanded.

"Yes, I stole it," Uncle Jake said. "But the girls had nothing to do with it."

"You are confessing to your crime?" the Little Mermaid said, surprised. "Most of the topsiders I have met are liars. Why would you admit your guilt and face almost certain death?"

"We need the blade to stop a Jabberwocky that is terrorizing the town," Uncle Jake said.

"Why would that concern me?" the mermaid said. "Let the monster destroy your town for all I care. Topsiders deserve no less! You are guilty! Feed them to the Cruel Crustacean!"

The guards seized the Grimms.

"Wait!" Uncle Jake cried. "There was another reason I did it."

"Let him speak," the princess said.

Uncle Jake stammered but then smiled and said, "I have a crush on you!"

Daphne stepped forward. "It's true. You're all he talks about."

"Twenty-four hours a day," Sabrina added nervously.

"He thinks you're a total hottie!" Daphne added as sincerely as she could. "He wants to marry you and have a million merbabies."

"You're pushing it a bit far," Uncle Jake muttered to the little girl.

"Is this true?" the princess said. Even in the dim underwater light Sabrina could see her blushing.

"I stole the blade because I wanted to meet you," Uncle Jake explained. "I have been all over the world and have seen a lot of women but the rumors of your beauty could not be ignored. I had to risk my life to see if those rumors were true."

"Nonsense." The princess giggled. "I've seen the celebrity magazines that float down here from your world. I know I'm not as thin as they are."

"Those women don't hold a candle to you," Uncle Jake replied. "Why, I bet if you came up to the surface you'd be in one of those magazines, too."

"Every word that comes out of your mouth is a filthy lie," the princess snapped. Sabrina gulped. It seemed as if Uncle Jake's plan had fallen apart, until the mermaid's face softened and a wide smile appeared. "And I love every single one of them."

Uncle Jake looked over at Sabrina and winked. Their uncle had his own magic inside him. He was one of the most charming men she had ever met.

"I know what I did was wrong, but I'm glad I did it. Too bad you're going to kill us, though. I would have loved to go back to the surface and tell that ex-boyfriend of yours how gorgeous you still are. He lives in town. I hear he lost all his hair and moved back in with his mom. He's pathetic. He got just what he deserved."

"You say he is miserable?"

"Oh, yes. Just a shell of the man he once was," Uncle Jake replied.

The Little Mermaid smiled. "I wish I could see his face when you tell him how great I am doing."

"I could take a picture and bring it back," Uncle Jake offered.

The princess giggled mischievously. "That's a very tempting offer."

"Since I would be going up there and coming back anyway, you could lend me your portion of the Vorpal blade. Once I'm done with it, I could bring it back to you with the picture and we can laugh at how stupid your loser ex looks."

The Little Mermaid and Uncle Jake laughed together.

"All right, you naughty boy," the princess said. "You've got yourself a deal. You are free to go and you can take the blade, too."

"Oh, I knew you would be wonderful!" Daphne said, clapping her hands. "I saw the movie they made about you. It was so romantic!"

Uncle Jake put his hand over the little girl's mouth but it was too late. The Little Mermaid's face turned red and contorted with anger.

"*Romantic*! Oh, yes, it was romantic. Unfortunately, *it never happened*! There was no happily ever after for me. He dumped me and ran off to marry some tart."

"But he's bald now, princess," Uncle Jake said. "Repugnant. Lives in his parents' basement. Remember?"

"He threw a lot of pretty words around but he didn't really mean them. He got my hopes up and then he left me for the first thing with feet that came along. But what should I have expected from a topsider? My parents tried to warn me. My sisters did, too. All topsiders are the same. They're nothing but a bunch of liars."

"Your majesty. It's obvious you are upset," Sabrina cried. "We'll just take the blade and go."

"As I suspected! You're not down here to give me compliments," the overstuffed princess growled. She reached over and seized the Vorpal blade piece. "All you want is this! *Feed them to the Cruel Crustacean!*"

The merman guards rushed to a huge wooden wheel that protruded from a nearby wall. Together they struggled to turn it, and as they did, the floor beneath the family disappeared and the Grimms sank into the waters below. They tried to swim back into the throne room, but a dozen vicious-looking merman guards blocked the way. Trapped, the family floated down to the sandy floor below and looked around.

"This is bad, right?" Sabrina said, eyeing the dark chamber they found themselves in. "Anything called the Cruel Crustacean can't be looking for a hug."

"Just stay close," Uncle Jake said.

"Look!" Daphne cried as an enormous creature took its first step into the light. It was as big as Granny Relda's house, with eight fat legs that ended in spikes. Its eyes protruded from two long, armlike stalks that wiggled back and forth. It had a massive shell on its back and when it took a step, the ground beneath the family rumbled. Sabrina recognized the monster for what it was. The Chinese restaurant on the corner near their apartment in Manhattan had a much smaller one in a tank by the register. It was a hermit crab, a *really big* hermit crab.

"Oh, I am going to have some really wicked nightmares after this," said Daphne.

Sabrina looked around the chamber. "There's nowhere to hide in here. What are we going to do?"

Uncle Jake took off his overcoat and dropped it at the girls' feet. "I'll fight this thing off as long as I can." He rushed forward, shouting at the ugly beast to distract it from the sisters.

Sabrina snatched her Uncle's overcoat and searched through

its pockets. "There's got to be something here that will help." She pulled out a red brooch with a black eye painted in the middle. She held it up and for a brief moment it glowed with power, but then it fizzled out. Sabrina grimaced and shoved it back into the pocket. She found a little black marble hidden in another pocket and threw it at the monster, hoping for some enormous explosion, but it bounced off the hermit crab's shell and was buried in the sand.

"What was that supposed to do?" Daphne asked.

"Beats me! I'm trying everything."

While Sabrina searched, Uncle Jake did his best to stay out of the way of the hermit crab's legs. It was no easy feat. The crab used them as impaling spikes, bringing them down hard and pulverizing the ground. If one of them connected with Uncle Jake, he'd be a goner.

"Let me help," Daphne said as she dug through the overcoat's pockets as well.

"I thought you said magic was bad," Sabrina said.

Daphne scowled at her sister and stuck her tongue out to give her a raspberry. Together they pulled out a variety of odd-colored rings, carved totems, voodoo dolls, and some amulets made from bones. They tried to activate each of the trinkets, but with zero knowledge of what they did or how to use them, they failed every time. Nothing was working, and the hermit crab had nearly made a shish kebab of their uncle.

"Look for something that gives you a jolt," Uncle Jake shouted. "You'll feel the magic if it's going to work down here."

Sabrina dug through more pockets, discarding anything that didn't feel powerful. Finally, she reached into a pocket and it felt as if something inside had given her an electrical shock.

"What are these?" Sabrina asked, yanking out a pair of slippers.

"The Shoes of Swiftness," Uncle Jake shouted. "Put them on!"

Sabrina eyed the slippers closely. "What do they do?"

Uncle Jake was too busy with the crab to answer, so Sabrina kicked off her shoes and pulled on the slippers. She immediately felt an energy, much like the one the Wand of Merlin gave her. It was incredible and powerful.

Just then, Uncle Jake cried out in pain. Sabrina spun around and found him up against a wall with nowhere to run and the crab raising a deadly spike to skewer him. There was no escape for him.

"No!" Sabrina said, instinctively running to his side, and as she did, something marvelous happened. Her feet moved so fast she was able to snatch her uncle out of the way of certain death. In a flash she and her uncle were standing next to a dumbfounded Daphne.

"OK, that was cool," Daphne admitted.

"I've got an idea," Sabrina said, staring up at the hole. "Grab on to my arms and hold on tight!" Daphne slipped her hand into her sister's. Uncle Jake reached down, grabbed his overcoat, and then slipped his free hand into Sabrina's. The Cruel Crustacean charged at them, but in the blink of an eye they were gone. Sabrina's legs became a blur and in no time the trio were propelled upward as if they were attached to a powerboat motor. They rocketed to freedom through the hole, shocking the merman guards. Sabrina spotted the Vorpal blade, still in the chubby hands of the mermaid princess, and darted in her direction. As they passed her, Uncle Jake snatched it away.

"Thanks, beautiful," he quipped.

The Little Mermaid screamed with rage and a gurgling alarm was sounded. A second later, Sabrina watched as the massive doors to the chamber began to close.

"They're trying to trap us inside!" Uncle Jake warned.

"Hang on!" Sabrina cried and started kicking, this time aiming for the narrowing gap between the doors. Again the group rocketed forward, just slipping through before the doors crushed them to death. They streaked across the main hall, out through the gate, and into the busy streets. Kicking as hard as she could, Sabrina propelled the family down the road, sending mermen and mermaids leaping out of their path. Once they were safely away from the palace, Sabrina angled toward the surface.

"Any idea where the boat is?" she said.

"Over there!" Daphne said, pointing to the bright orange anchor they had tossed over the side.

"I recommend we get there as fast as we can," Uncle Jake said, pointing below. Sabrina looked down and saw an army of angry merman guards swimming toward them. Following on their heels was the enormous hermit crab.

Sabrina kicked faster toward the surface. Unfortunately, she misjudged the power of her feet and the group exploded out of the water, flying fifteen feet into the air. A moment later they came crashing back down into the river. Uncle Jake was the first to struggle to the surface again. He pulled Daphne and Sabrina over to the boat and they all climbed in. Uncle Jake snatched up the oars and rowed furiously, but they'd forgotten to pull up the anchor; it held them in place.

"I can't breathe!" Daphne cried suddenly. Uncle Jake dropped the oars and yanked the sticky starfish off the little girl's head with a *slurp*! Daphne gasped at first but soon she was breathing fine and helped Sabrina pull off her own starfish. Uncle Jake shoved his into his overcoat.

"Might come in handy someday," he said, as he began to pull up the heavy anchor.

The first wave of merman soldiers leaped out of the water like dolphins, flapping their tails back and forth to stay above the surface. They were several yards away from the boat but held their tridents menacingly as they approached the family. A second wave of soldiers appeared behind them, followed by the rising shell of the giant hermit crab. It opened its ugly mouth and a high-pitched scream erupted from its throat. When the first trident struck the side of the boat, Sabrina knew they had to do something, and fast. She leaped to her feet, snatched a length of the anchor rope, and moved to the back of the little boat.

"What are you doing?" Uncle Jake said as he finally dragged the anchor out of the water.

"I have absolutely no idea," Sabrina said and she took off toward the front of the boat and leaped onto the water. Her legs were going a mile a minute, so fast Sabrina couldn't even see her own feet. Each step was so quick she found she could run on top of the water as if it were pavement. She raced across the surface of the Hudson River toward the shore. With the rope in hand she dragged the boat behind her, leaving a powerful wake that built up strength and slammed into the merman army like a tidal wave.

When she reached the shore, she was so excited that she kept on running up the embankment, across some train tracks, narrowly missing the express to Grand Central Station, and into the forest where she finally came to a stop. Sabrina's feet felt like they were on fire. She kicked the magic slippers off as quickly as she could. The energy that they had given her quickly faded, and suddenly, she wanted to put them back on even though she knew they would burn her feet. She was about to actually do it when Uncle Jake handed her the Wand of Merlin.

"I found this in the bottom of the boat," he said.

Sabrina snatched it away, surprised by how greedily she wanted it. The magic swirled through her and she smiled. Daphne gave her a startled, disapproving look but she ignored it.

"Well, that's two out of three," Uncle Jake said, holding up the piece of the broken sword. He looked down at the inscription on it.

BEG THE HAG OF THE HILLS, it read.

• • •

Sabrina dipped a washcloth into the bowl of cool water that sat next to Puck's bed and wrung it out. Then she patted it across the boy's fevered brow. He mumbled incoherently for a few moments and then went back to sleep.

Granny and Uncle Jake were in the living room, busily searching the journals for references to a "hag of the hills," while Daphne had long since surrendered to sleep and was napping in a rocking chair next to the bed. It was late, and though Sabrina knew a cup of coffee would keep her awake, the bitter taste wasn't worth it. Instead, she found that by lightly touching the Wand of Merlin in her pocket, she got enough of a jolt of energy to completely refresh her. She wanted to look after Puck in case he woke and needed something.

A wave of emotions overtook her—emotions she didn't understand: genuine concern for the boy, anger at his recklessness, confusion at the memory of their kiss. She felt like crying when she realized how vicious her rejection of him had been.

"Hey, stink-bottom," Sabrina said, wondering if the boy could hear her. If he could, he'd never let her live down any kind words she might say to him. Besides, trading insults with her seemed to be his favorite game. Maybe it would make him feel better deep down.

"You realize you're a terrible burden on all of us. Look at you lying in that bed. You're not fooling anyone. I'd bet a hundred bucks that you're faking all of this just for the attention. Well, your pampering is about to come to an end, buster. When we have all the pieces of the Vorpal blade, we're going to find the Blue Fairy and put them back together. Once we kill the Jabberwocky, Red Riding Hood will be no problem. Mom and Dad will come home and then we're shipping you off to the Faerie folk. You'll be back to being a pain in my butt in no time at all."

She looked over at her sister to make sure she was still sleeping, too, and then removed the wand from her pocket. She laid it on the bed and examined it with awe. Just having it near made her feel like everything was going to be fine. She could handle everything herself. Puck would live and she'd bring her parents home. Nothing could get in her way.

"Are you OK?" Daphne asked.

"I'm fine," Sabrina said, snatching the wand off the bed and stuffing it back into her pocket.

"You were staring at that thing for fifteen minutes," Daphne said. "I said your name a few times but you didn't hear me."

Sabrina shot a glance at the clock on the wall. Her sister was right. "I have a lot on my mind."

"I want you to give that thing to Granny," Daphne insisted. "It belongs in the mirror where it will be safe."

"It'll be safe with me."

Daphne got out of her chair and crossed the room. She stood over Sabrina and looked at her closely. "But are you going to be safe from it?"

"You're being silly."

"No, I'm not," the little girl said a bit too loudly. "I saw your face when you used the wand. It was the same face you had when you used the shoes."

"What face is that?"

"You looked like you wanted to hurt someone," Daphne said.

"No, what I looked like is someone who isn't afraid anymore," Sabrina said. "Daphne, aren't you sick to death of running all the time?"

"The first thing I learned in Ms. White's self-defense class is that there are things that you stand and fight and there are things that you run from. A smart warrior knows the difference. You used to know the difference."

"You know, when I woke up in the hospital you claimed that I didn't include you in things anymore," Sabrina complained. "Did you ever think that the reason is because everything I do is wrong in your eyes?'

"We are still a team," Daphne said. "And you are still wrong. You're getting add . . . add . . . what's that word Granny said earlier?"

"Addicted?"

"Yes, addicted."

"Whatever."

"Don't you 'whatever' me!"

They sat in silence and eventually Daphne got up from her chair. "I'm going to bed."

"Fine," Sabrina said, still angry at her sister's accusation.

"Be careful, Sabrina," Daphne whispered and she stepped out of the room.

• • •

A loud, raspy breath woke Sabrina from her sleep. The room was dark and a girlish giggle sent Sabrina dashing to the light switch. She flipped it on and realized at once that she wasn't in her grandmother's room anymore. She was in her own bed and standing by it was the Jabberwocky and Red Riding Hood. Sabrina reached into her pocket and took out the Wand of Merlin. She aimed it at the monster and thought about big bolts of lightning rocking the sky.

"How did you get in here?" she asked.

The little girl laughed. "Silly."

"Where are my parents?" Sabrina demanded, eyeing Daphne. She was sound asleep and snoring heavily. Daphne could sleep through a war.

"They're safe. I've got my grandmother now and my doggy."

"You lie!"

The little girl giggled.

"Granny!" Sabrina shouted, but the old woman didn't reply. *"Mr. Canis!"* There was no sound.

"All I need is one more member of my family before we can play house. I need a little sister," Red Riding Hood said. Sabrina gasped and the Jabberwocky took a step toward Daphne's slumbering body.

"No!" Sabrina cried and a flash of light exploded through the window. It hit the Jabberwocky in the back and knocked it to its knees.

"Stop!" Red Riding Hood cried. "You'll kill my kitty!"

Sabrina didn't care. She scampered out of bed as another bolt hit the downed beast. It screeched in pain. Dozens more blasts lit up the room. The Jabberwocky cried out as each one fried it with white hot light. To Sabrina, the cries sounded like pleas for mercy, but she wouldn't listen. She wanted this thing dead and soon she got her wish. The monster slumped to the ground, gasped, and was still.

Red Riding Hood rushed to the Jabberwocky's body and cried in despair.

"You killed her!"

Sabrina smiled in triumph. She walked over to get a better view, but was surprised to find the monster was no longer there. Its massive, smoldering carcass had been replaced with the body of young girl with blonde hair. Stunned, Sabrina dropped to her knees to see the girl's face. She brushed away the hair and gasped. "It's me!"

Sabrina turned to the mirror in her room and nearly screamed when she saw her reflection. Her legs were gone, replaced with hulking clawed feet. She looked down at them and noticed that she also had a long reptilian tail. It swung around the room uncontrollably, destroying the little desk and dresser. Her arms had become a scaly mass of muscles and tendons with razor sharp talons on her fingertips. She screamed for someone to help her but no one came. She was turning into the Jabberwocky. She was becoming a monster and no one could help.

"They tried to warn you," Red Riding Hood said. She laughed maniacally as she put a huge leash around Sabrina's neck. "Come on, kitty. Let's play."

"Sabrina!" a voice shouted. She felt someone's hand gently shaking her shoulder. She looked over and saw Granny Relda's concerned face.

"You were having a nightmare," she said.

Sabrina looked down at her body. It was back to normal. She had had another of her awful dreams.

"Are you OK?" her grandmother asked.

Sabrina nodded.

"Well, put on something warm. Your uncle and I have discovered who the hag of the hills is," Granny Relda said.

"Good! Where's Uncle Jake?" Sabrina asked as she got up.

"He's downstairs having a drink," the old woman said.

"A drink? Why?"

"To calm his nerves, I suppose. He's not too exited about who has the last piece of the Vorpal blade."

"I don't understand," Sabrina said. "Who's got the last piece?"

"The witch," Granny said. "The one they call Baba Yaga."

9

Sabrina had heard many stories about Baba Yaga and read even more. What she knew was disturbing. Baba Yaga was thousands of years old and it was rumored that she was a cannibal. Many of the family journals described heart-stopping encounters with her. They talked of her home, decorated with the bones of her latest meal. She seemed like an odd ally for the Grimm family, but time and time again the family had turned to her for help.

Baba Yaga was responsible for the barrier that kept the Everafters in Ferryport Landing, but nothing she did came without a price. As payment for the spell, Baba Yaga had stolen the Grimm family's freedom forever. A Grimm would have to stay in the town as long as the barrier existed.

"So she eats people?" Daphne whispered to her sister in the backseat of the car as they drove to see the witch. Her arms were wrapped around Elvis as if he were a life preserver and she was lost at sea.

Sabrina nodded. "That's the story."

"That's so gross," Daphne said. She hugged the Great Dane. "Don't let anybody eat me, Elvis."

Elvis whined, then turned his attention to a paper sack Granny had given them for the trip. Granny had stayed behind with Puck and said they would need whatever was inside to get to the witch.

Uncle Jake was silent and pale as he drove the car along the road that snaked across Mount Taurus. The girls tried to ask him more about the witch. After all, he had come face to face with her and survived, but he seemed to be in a different world. Sabrina reached into her pocket and clutched the Wand of Merlin. A little charge raced through her and made her nervousness vanish.

We'll be just fine, she told herself. *And if we aren't, that old lunatic is going to regret it.*

Suddenly Uncle Jake pulled over to the side of the road and parked the car.

"Why are we stopping?" Sabrina said, glancing out the window at the dense, snow-covered forest. The trees that lined the road looked black, even in the morning sunlight, as if their life force had been sucked out of them.

"We're here," Uncle Jake replied. He looked out the car window into the woods and cracked his knuckles nervously.

Daphne stared out the window. "Where's here?"

Jake ignored her question. "You two stay in the car. I'll be right back."

"What?" the girls cried.

"I'll be back soon."

"No way!" Sabrina cried. "We're going with you."

"It's too dangerous," Uncle Jake said. "Trust me, girls. If I didn't have to go, I wouldn't. The last time I ran into Baba Yaga she told me she'd skin me and eat me as jerky. It's best if you wait in the car."

"I can't believe you!" Sabrina complained. "You're treating us like a couple of little kids!"

"Uh, we are a couple of little kids," Daphne said.

Sabrina ignored her. "We've seen bigger trouble than this Baba Yaga lady. We killed a giant. We stopped Rumpelstiltskin. Why, a couple of hours ago I rescued us all from a hermit crab as big as a house. We're going."

Sabrina opened the door, got out of the car, and turned to her sister, "Come on."

"Fine, but if we get turned into jerky, I'm telling Granny," the little girl grumbled, getting out of the car and pulling Elvis with her.

"Just stay close, then," Uncle Jake said.

"Wait! The bag!" Daphne said. She crawled back into the car and grabbed the paper sack, then rejoined the group.

Elvis led the way through the woods. They journeyed deeper and deeper into the forest, through glades that were deadly quiet. The trees were closely packed, as if huddling together might save them from something. The Grimms could feel an odd creepiness around them, as if they were being watched. Every twig that snapped or bird that whistled caused Uncle Jake to jump. Sabrina noticed he was sweating even in the frigid winter air.

They soon found a path made up of white oval stones that stuck up from the ground at different angles, making it difficult to walk. Daphne quickly lost her footing and fell to her knees. As Sabrina helped her up, the little girl screamed.

"What?" Uncle Jake stammered.

"Look!" Daphne cried as she pointed down at the path. Sabrina bent down and brushed some snow off one of the white stones and her heart stopped. The path wasn't made of stones at all. It was a collection of human skulls all looking up at them with horrible grins of death.

"Gross!" Daphne shouted.

"At least we know we're getting close," Sabrina said.

"That's what they all thought, too!" Uncle Jake said.

Just then, a bright orange cat appeared. It stood on the path hissing and baring its fangs. Elvis growled menacingly but the cat was not impressed.

"Let's go back," Uncle Jake said.

"What? Why?" Sabrina said. "It's a cat!"

"It's not a cat," her uncle argued.

"Come on, stop being silly," Sabrina said as she walked toward the angry feline. Much to her surprise, the cat changed with every step she took toward it. It grew and morphed until it was a creature somewhere between a tiger and a man. Sabrina stared up at it and reached for her wand, but Daphne rushed over and yanked her back to the group. With every step backward the creature morphed back into the cat.

"Okay, so it's not a cat," Sabrina said as she tried to catch her breath.

"His name is Bright Sun," Uncle Jake said. "You could say he's one of Baba Yaga's bodyguards."

Suddenly, there was a low growl behind them. The group spun around and found a little black terrier on the path behind them. A high-pitched shriek from above sent their gaze upward to a red-tailed hawk landing on a tree limb over their heads.

"We're being attacked by a pet store," Sabrina grumbled.

"The dog is Black Midnight and the bird is Red Dawn. They want an offering before we can pass."

Sabrina pulled Merlin's wand out of her pocket. "Well, I have a solution to this problem."

"Uh, hello?" Daphne said as she shook the paper sack. "Granny gave us this for a reason. Maybe there's something in here that can help that doesn't require you to blow anything up."

The little girl opened the sack and her face curled up in revulsion. She reached inside and took out a small, brown mouse. It was dead. Daphne tossed it to the ground and the hawk swooped down and snatched it in its sharp talons. Daphne reached into the sack again and pulled out a can of sardines. She turned the key and rolled back the lid, then set the can on the ground. Bright Sun bounded toward it and ate the little fish hungrily. Finally, Daphne took a small rubber bone out of the sack. She squeezed it and it squeaked loudly. She tossed the bone to the terrier, who caught it in his mouth and chewed happily. Then, without a sound, the three animals stepped off the path.

"Looks like Granny is right," Daphne said. "You don't need magic to solve everything."

Sabrina shrugged, put the wand back in her pocket, and the family continued farther down the path.

Soon they came to a clearing where a small one-story shack stood. A little white fence encircled the yard and made the house look quaint, as if it were a summer cottage in need of a bit of tender loving care. But as Sabrina got closer she got a jolt of surprise. The fence was actually made from bleached human bones. The yard was full of broken cauldrons and animal skeletons, including the skull of a catlike animal with massive tusks. The house had a heavy wooden door on the front and two little windows that looked like eyes staring down at them. If Sabrina hadn't known better, she would have thought the house was scowling at them.

She opened the gate, stepped into the yard, and walked to the front door. A wind chime on the fence clinked as it caught a soft breeze. Sabrina examined the chimes. They were made from dried ears and rusty screws. She cringed. "Don't look," Sabrina said.

"We won't," Daphne and Uncle Jake replied from far off. Sabrina turned to see her little sister, her uncle, and Elvis still cowering at the gate.

"Come on!" she said, reaching into her pocket for a boost from her wand. "Don't be a bunch of cowards."

"I've got a bad feeling about this," Daphne said as she and the group took a hesitant step into the yard.

Sabrina knocked on the heavy door but there was no reply. She knocked again with the same results.

"Maybe she's out," Daphne said.

"Out? Where is she going to go? She's a witch," Sabrina argued.

"Maybe she's at the witch grocery store. I don't know," Daphne said testily.

"There's no such thing as a witch grocery store," Sabrina argued. Her little sister was getting on her nerves.

"Girls!" Uncle Jake shouted. "Let's just go in and get this over with. If she's not home, then we'll search for the sword and count our blessings that we didn't have to see her."

Sabrina pushed on the door and it opened. "Stay together," she said to the group as she stepped inside. Immediately, Sabrina felt her body tingling. Magic was all around her. She scanned the room and found it filled with old jars and buckets of icky black goop. There was a table off to the side littered with ancient books and odd potions that bubbled and hissed. The floor was filthy and the only light source was a roaring fire in the fireplace.

A crud-covered chandelier hung from the ceiling and there were little dried apples on the fireplace mantel. A door on the opposite wall was ajar but from where they were standing they couldn't see what might be on the other side. Sabrina stepped over to the table and picked up one of the enormous books. Inside she found the scrawls of a shaky hand, describing mysterious incantations in both English and a language she had never seen before. Something inside her wanted to speak the words out loud. She was sure something amazing would happen. She flipped through more pages and realized the paper felt odd on her fingertips. It felt almost alive. She looked at it closely and realized little hairs were sticking out of it. It was made from skin! She dropped the book and took a step backward, only to feel a blast of intense heat from the fireplace behind her. She spun around and saw the flame reaching out to her. She could have sworn there were faces in the fire—faces that cried out for mercy and freedom.

Suddenly, there was a horrible scream. It had come from

behind the door of a neighboring room. Everyone froze. Uncle Jake looked like he was going to be sick. They crept toward the door and pushed it open. Gathering all her courage, Sabrina stepped inside.

There was Baba Yaga. The crusty looking woman had dry gray hair and a long pointy nose. Her fingernails were nearly as long as her arms and her face was wrinkled and scarred. She had one milky white eye that seemed to look in a different direction than the other, and her teeth were sharp in a way that could have only happened by filing them down. She was sitting in a chair made of bones and animal skins watching a soap opera on her television.

"Welcome, Grimms. I'm sorry. I didn't hear you knock," she said in a thick Russian accent. She grinned and gestured to her TV. "I get so caught up in my stories. Hope just caught Bo having an affair with Marlena. You should have heard her scream. It was hilarious. But, that's what Hope gets. She was cheating on Bo with John when they went to Spain. Now's not the time to get on the moral high-horse."

The family stared at the witch, dumbfounded.

"You've never seen *Days of Our Lives*?" she asked.

Everyone shook their heads.

"Oh, well," the witch said as she was lifted out of the chair and placed on the floor by an unseen force. "Relda has told me about your problem. I believe I can be of some assistance."

"So, you're not going to eat us?" Daphne said.

"Not today, child. Perhaps when you are older. Children are mostly gristle at your age," Baba Yaga said as she turned to Jake. "But you, on the other hand. I thought I told you I would feast on your innards the next time I saw you in my house."

Uncle Jake shuddered. "We need your part of the Vorpal blade," he stammered. "I wouldn't have come if it wasn't important."

"You Grimm men are a bit jumpy. Spaulding Grimm was the same way when he brought me the blade," she said. "What's the matter, Jacob? Do I make you nervous?"

Sabrina clutched the wand in her pocket and stepped forward bravely.

"Are you going to give us the blade or not?" she said.

"For a price," the witch said.

"A price?" Sabrina said.

"There is always a price, child."

"OK, what do you want?" Sabrina said, reaching into her other pocket. She pulled out a couple dollars in change. She urged her sister to do the same. Daphne managed to produce a little rubber ball, a button, a paper clip, and ten cents. "I suppose if this isn't enough, we could mow your lawn in the summertime, maybe dust your bones and headstones."

"I want the wand," Baba Yaga said.

The words felt like a slap in the face to Sabrina. For the last few days, she had felt confident like never before and it was all due to Merlin's wand. When she had it in her hand, she no longer had to run. Bad guys backed away. It was the source of her power and it dissolved her fear. Asking her to give up the wand was like asking her to hand over a leg or an arm.

"I don't know what you're talking about," she lied.

The witch smiled broadly, revealing a mouth full of puffy gums. "The child has been touched, Jacob," she said, eyeing the man. "Just like her uncle."

"No, she hasn't," Uncle Jake said with a sneer as he turned to Sabrina. "Give it to her, 'Brina."

"No," Sabrina said. "We might need it when we face Red Riding Hood and the Jabberwocky."

"No wand, no blade. It's that simple," Baba Yaga said.

Sabrina took the wand out of her pocket and pointed it at the old woman. Her hand was shaking with anger. "Then we'll take it from you!"

"Sabrina, think about Mom and Dad. We need the blade, not

some lousy magic stick," Daphne pleaded, but was drowned out by the rumbling thunder overhead.

"Sabrina, give the wand to Baba Yaga!" Uncle Jake shouted.

Sabrina shook her head. "Give us the blade!"

The witch cocked an eyebrow at her and sneered. "You don't want me as your enemy, child."

Suddenly, Uncle Jake reached into his pocket and removed a small fire-red stone. Energy emanated from it and filled the room, and suddenly a shocking force yanked the wand out of Sabrina's hands, sending it sailing across the room and into Baba Yaga's hand. The energy running through Sabrina quickly faded, only to be replaced with a rage at her uncle for betraying her.

"OK, old mother," Uncle Jake said. "You've got your payment. Let's see the merchandise."

"Very well," the witch said as she stepped across the room to a table where an old mug sat that read FOXY GRANDMA. It was filled with wands. She carelessly stuffed Sabrina's in with the others and opened a drawer in the table. Inside was a shiny piece of metal. She took it out and handed the piece of blade to Jake.

He studied it. Sabrina noticed that unlike the other portions of the blade, there was no inscription carved into it. There was no clue to finding the Blue Fairy.

"We need help putting this back together," Uncle Jake said.

"The Blue Fairy is the only one who can do it. If the price was right, could you tell us where she is?"

The old crone shook her head. Mounds of hair fell from her head and onto the floor. "Some things are not for sale," the witch said. She clapped her hands and Red Dawn, Bright Sun, and Dark Midnight entered the room.

"My knights will escort you out," Baba Yaga said.

Jake nodded to her respectfully and led the girls toward the door.

"Well, that was easier than I expected," Uncle Jake said.

"Jacob," the old witch called out. "Your mother saved you from my hungry teeth this time. She paid quite a price for your past intrusion. You should go home and thank her. But know this: If you ever invade my home again, I'll suck the marrow out of your bones while you watch."

Uncle Jake's face turned white and Elvis let out a surprised yelp.

"Tell your mother I said hello," Baba Yaga continued, changing her tone to that of a sweet old lady. The cat, the hawk, and the terrier led the family outside into the cold clearing and left them at the gate.

Uncle Jake looked down at the blade and smiled. "We did it!"

Daphne hugged Elvis tightly. "You were so brave!"

"Let's get this home and see what Mom has to say about it," Uncle Jake said.

"No," Sabrina said softly. "I can't leave the wand with her. It belongs to me and we need it. You saw her. She tossed it aside like it was nothing. Well, it's not nothing! That wand might save our lives."

"Sabrina, get ahold of yourself," Uncle Jake snapped. "We've got the blade. That's what's important. We're lucky all she wanted was the wand. It's gone. Forget about it."

Sabrina couldn't believe he was so willing to surrender. Before her uncle could stop her, she reached into his overcoat pocket and snatched the Shoes of Swiftness. She slipped them on and turned to her family. "I'm going back for it! She won't even know I was in there."

"Sabrina, no!" Uncle Jake demanded, but it was too late. Sabrina ran back to the house, opened the door, and in a flash she was racing into Baba Yaga's room. She snatched the mug off the little table at a speed faster than the human eye. Unfortunately, Baba Yaga stuck out a bony leg and tripped her. Sabrina slammed hard onto the floor and the little mug shattered, spraying magic wands all over the floor. Sabrina snatched up the nearest one before being yanked off her feet by her hair. Baba Yaga's inhuman strength allowed her to dangle Sabrina in front of her.

"Your grandmother would be disappointed to know you are a thief," the witch said. "Cooking you would save her the anguish of finding out."

Sabrina fumbled with the wand and eventually aimed it at the witch's face. She thought of thunderstorms and flicked the wand with her wrist. Nothing happened.

The witch cackled. "I'll give you some credit. You're braver than your uncle. He snuck in here and ran like a rat when I found him. You're still putting up a fight. Sadly, your passion is fueled by your addiction. It's made you so blind you can't even tell that you're not holding Merlin's wand. All that little trinket does is turn people into frogs."

"Well, then I hope you like flies, ugly," Sabrina said as she conjured a big fat, slimy frog in her mind. There was a sudden zap and a cloud of dust and the sound of laughter filled her ears.

"You really have to be sure to point those things in the right direction," the witch said as the smoke cleared. Sabrina was no longer in the witch's grasp; in fact, she was staring directly at the woman's crusty, corny feet.

Fudge, I made her a giant, Sabrina thought to herself as Baba Yaga's gnarled hand reached down and scooped her off the floor. Sabrina squirmed but she couldn't get free.

"Oh, goodie for me," the witch said as she held Sabrina close to her face. "I haven't had frog legs since the last time I was in Paris."

Frog legs? What is she talking about? Sabrina looked down at herself. Her feet were green and webbed. Her skin was slimy and sticky. Her belly was like a massive sack hanging between her skinny little legs. A bubbling gurgle churned in her gut, slowly rising up through her body, and then her wide mouth opened. "I'm a frog!" she croaked.

Baba Yaga lifted the frog girl above her head and slowly dipped her down into her open jaws. Sabrina struggled and used her webbed feet to block her descent into the witch's hungry mouth. Wiggling frantically, she slipped out of the witch's hand and tumbled to the floor. Without allowing herself any time to recover, she leaped toward the door, flailing and screaming as she went. Her new amphibious body could leap incredible lengths but controlling the leaps was impossible.

"My lunch!" the witch cried. "She's getting away! Red Dawn, Bright Sun, Dark Midnight . . . help Mommy!"

The animals raced into the room. They spotted Sabrina and raced after her. She jumped as hard as she could, and her skinny springlike legs propelled her high over the creatures' sharp claws and vicious fangs. She sailed into the next room. Spotting the front door on the opposite wall, she jumped toward it but unfortunately smacked into it headfirst. She fell, dazed and hurt, as the witch's guardians rushed toward her. All three began to grow and change. Bright Sun returned to his tiger-warrior form, while Red Dawn morphed into a horrible birdlike man with a savage beak and rippling arms. Black Midnight's transformation was equally disturbing. When it was finished, he was a hunched, muscled giant with thick black hair all over his body and savage fangs. All three of the guardians were in armor and held long swords in their hands.

Sabrina hopped onto the table with the witch's potions and powders, knocking over vials and bowls. The three guardians swung their swords at her frog body, destroying books with each mighty blow. Sabrina managed to keep just ahead of the knights, but she couldn't hop forever.

Bright Sun landed a blow that nearly took off her webbed foot and managed to upend a bowl, splattering himself with a particularly foul-smelling potion. He was instantly transformed into a little red mouse. He scurried across the floor, but not before he caught the attention of Red Dawn. The hawk-man dove for the mouse, only to morph into a tiny spider when he knocked a vial of blue powder on himself. Black Midnight kept up the chase, but quickly suffered a similar fate as his companions. Something spilled on him that made his body inflate like a balloon. He soon drifted to the ceiling where he was unable to get at Sabrina.

Sabrina leaped back down to the ground and headed for the closed door. She soon realized that without hands to open it she was trapped inside the house.

"Uncle Jake!" she cried "Open the door!"

Suddenly, the door swung open and Sabrina hopped out into the cold air. The family stared down at her with mouths agape.

"All right, let me say it for you: 'I told you so!'" Sabrina grumbled.

"Is that you?" Uncle Jake said, reaching down and picking her up off the ground.

"Yes," she said. "You're squeezing too hard."

Just then, a window opened and the witch stuck her head out of it. She shook her fist at the family and screamed.

"She's mine," Baba Yaga shouted from a window. "She tried to steal from me!"

"You know I can't give her back, crone," Uncle Jake said.

"I was hoping you'd say that," the witch said. A liquidy cackle bubbled from her throat and the ground started to shake.

"What's that?" Daphne said.

"Here, hold your sister," Uncle Jake said as he put Sabrina into Daphne's hands. He nervously fumbled through his pockets, yanking out odds and ends and growing more discouraged by the second.

"What's going on?" Sabrina said, struggling for a view around Daphne's thumb. Uncle Jake turned to her and tried to explain, but his words were drowned out by a horrible tearing sound followed by an incredible sight. Baba Yaga's house lifted itself off the ground on two massive chicken legs. It walked toward them. Sabrina wanted to scream but all that came out was "Ribbit!" Daphne and Elvis both whined at the same time.

"You know what?" Uncle Jake said, giving up his search. "Let's just make a run for it." He spun around, snatched Daphne's free hand, and dragged her back down the path. Elvis followed, barking and growling at the house that stomped after them.

"I hope you're happy," Daphne said to Sabrina as the group raced through the woods. "When we find Mom and Dad, I'm telling!"

The dense forest slowed the house down a little, but with each step its sharp chicken claws got closer and closer, eventually snagging the back of Uncle Jake's overcoat. Desperate, he slipped out of the coat and left it behind.

The house stopped abruptly and lowered itself to the ground. Baba Yaga popped out of the front door, scurried over to the overcoat, and snatched it up in her gnarled hands. She riffled through the pockets and let out a laugh that echoed through the woods. Sabrina turned her little frog head and saw Baba Yaga holding the final piece of the sword high in the air above her head. Her heart sank. They'd been so close to recovering the third piece of the blade and she'd ruined it. Why couldn't she just let the old woman have the wand? Why had she been so reckless?

But then the witch did something incredible. She tossed the blade through the air. It landed at Uncle Jake's feet. "You forgot your prize, Jacob!" she shouted, then held up his overcoat. "I'll take this as payment for the child's thieving ways," she said as she rolled it into a ball. She went back into her house and the gigantic chicken legs lifted it once again. Awkawardly, it turned itself around, and then lumbered back the way it came.

"Uncle Jake, I'm so sorry," Sabrina said. "It's my fault you lost all your magic."

"What's important is we have the last piece of the blade," Daphne said. "Uncle Jake can find a new coat."

"Except I did have a magic potion in my inside pocket we could have used to de-frog Sabrina," their uncle said.

"What am I going to do?" Sabrina groaned.

"I think you should stay like that for awhile and think about how you're behaving," Daphne said.

"I absolutely agree," a voice said from nearby. The group turned and found Mr. Canis lurking in the trees.

"Mom sent you to check up on us, huh?" Uncle Jake said, sounding offended.

Canis ignored the question. He approached the group and stared down at Sabrina, who was still resting in her sister's hands.

"How did you get into this situation?" he said.

"She went back in for the Wand of Merlin," Daphne said. Sabrina looked up at her and flashed an angry look.

"And how did you come across the Wand of Merlin?" Mr. Canis growled, studying Uncle Jake.

"Uh, I gave it to her," Uncle Jake admitted.

The old man' eyes were aglow with anger. "The child is eleven years old. Grown men can't handle that kind of magic."

"He was trying to prepare us for the future," Sabrina said.

"You and I will have words later, child," Mr. Canis barked. "For now, we need to find a way to change you back."

"Why don't we just take her home? Mom is sure to know something in the Hall of Wonders that will fix her," Uncle Jake said.

Mr. Canis turned on Uncle Jake and grabbed him roughly by the collar. "Ever since you were a child you have been nothing but a problem for her. Every mess you made you expected your mother to clean up for you! Well, look at the mess you've made this time!"

"It's a simple frog-spell," Uncle Jake cried. "She's not hurt."

"I'm not talking about the spell! Sabrina risked her life and the safety of her family for a stupid piece of magic wood *you* gave her. The child is touched. She is addicted and you are to blame!"

"Mr. Canis," Daphne said setting her hand on his arm. "It's OK."

The child's comforting words had a soothing effect on the old man.

"This kind of spell can be broken with the kiss of someone with royal blood. Puck would have been perfect but he's still very ill," Mr. Canis said.

Sabrina wondered if anyone could tell when a frog blushed. She hoped not.

"Well, this town is crawling with princes," Uncle Jake said. "Who should we call?"

"Unfortunately, I am going to have to clean up this mess myself," Mr. Canis said. "Jacob, you're forcing me to ask a favor of my bitterest enemy."

"Absolutely not!" Sabrina cried when she realized whom he meant.

• • •

"Absolutely not!" Mayor Charming bellowed.

"It's the only way," Mr. Canis growled.

Charming looked around his mansion as if he were searching for an escape route. The entire house had become his campaign headquarters and signs blocked most of the windows. When he realized he was stuck, he scowled. "The Big Bad Wolf is asking for my help? The Devil must have his long underwear on today."

The two stared at each other in disgust. They had a long history and none of it was nice. Most of the time when the two got together, Granny Relda had to separate them like two schoolboys bent on fist fighting.

"You can do it on your own or you can do it with a substantial bite taken out of you," Mr. Canis threatened. "Your choice."

"I liked you better when you were dead," Charming said through gritted teeth. He stepped over to Daphne, who held out Sabrina in her hands. "Personally, I think the girl looks better this way. The mustache and goatee were unsettling. She's rather striking as a frog."

"Mayor, if you don't do this, I will follow you wherever you go. I will be your shadow until you relent. You will never escape me. Your scent is one I know well," Canis said.

"Fine," Charming said, rolling his eyes and picking Sabrina up out of her sister's hands. "I suppose you'll be registered voters eventually. Remember who did you a favor once."

He raised Sabrina's frog body to his face, closed his eyes, and planted a tiny peck on the top of her head. Sabrina felt the spell break immediately. There was a puff of smoke and when it was clear she looked down, saw that her feet and hands were normal, and almost started dancing with happiness.

The mayor, on the other hand, looked as if he might barf and quickly wiped his mouth with a handkerchief.

"Mayor, you're so cool," Daphne said, racing over to him and wrapping him in a big hug. He struggled to free himself but the little girl wouldn't let go. "I hope you win the election."

Charming smiled slightly and then managed to push away the affectionate little girl. "Well, you don't have to worry about that. The latest polls are in and I'm going to win by a landslide. If all goes well, I think our friend the Queen of Hearts is in for a very rude awakening." He stepped over and pinned "VOTE FOR CHARMING" buttons on everyone's coats. When he got to

Mr. Canis, he just set it in his hand. "Remember, vote early and vote often."

Mr. Canis squeezed the button hard and when he opened his hand the pin was crunched into the size of a dime. He dropped it on the floor without a word.

"Well, not that this wasn't fun, but it wasn't. You can find your own way out," the mayor said, sticking his face in the old man's. "Don't forget to take your dog with you."

Charming turned to Daphne and noticed Elvis at her side. "Both of them," he said. He ushered them out of his house a little bit more roughly than was polite, and slammed the door.

"Are you going to tell Granny what I did?" Sabrina asked Mr. Canis.

Mr. Canis scowled. "The disrespect you have for that woman is outrageous. Do you think she doesn't know every step you make? Every night you have left her house and disobeyed her she has known. I have followed you two children all over this town since the day you arrived. Your grandmother is not stupid."

The old man's eyes flared with anger and then he darted into the woods behind Charming's house.

10

he family gathered at the dining room table with the three pieces of the sword. Without one of Spaulding's hints, they were stumped as to how to find the Blue Fairy.

"Maybe the witch tricked us," Sabrina said bitterly as she picked up the final piece and studied it closely. "Maybe this isn't the real blade."

Uncle Jake took the sword piece and flipped it over. His face suddenly grew red and he slammed the metal down on the table. "We've been on a wild goose chase!" he said. "We've been wasting our time all along!"

Sabrina was surprised by his outburst.

Granny picked up the broken sword piece. "It's not a fake. This is part of the Vorpal blade."

"Well, a lot of good it's going to do us!" Uncle Jake shouted. He jumped up from his chair and stormed out of the room. A moment later they heard the front door slam. Sabrina went to follow, but Granny took her arm. "It's the magic, Sabrina. His pockets were filled with all kinds of things. He's going to have a short temper until he gets over his addiction to it all."

Sabrina nodded. She went to the closet and put on her coat, then pulled an old blanket off the top shelf, and went outside.

Uncle Jake was pacing back and forth on the front porch. The sun was rising but its rays had little effect on the sharp, cold air.

"Are you OK?" she asked.

"I'm just frustrated, 'Brina. We were so close to fixing everything," Uncle Jake said. "Now we're back at a dead end and there's nothing I can do about it. I hate feeling helpless."

Sabrina handed him the old blanket. Without his overcoat he was shivering. He wrapped it around his shoulders. "Thanks," he said.

"This is about more than just saving my mom and dad, isn't it?" Sabrina asked.

Uncle Jake nodded. "Mr. Canis was absolutely right. I was a

problem to my parents from day one. I never listened to them. I snuck out. I got into all kinds of trouble. I was stubborn and thought I knew everything."

"You sound a lot like me," Sabrina admitted.

"But I was wrong, 'Brina, and my dad died because of it. The Jabberwocky killed him because I set it free. It was one stupid decision that happened twelve years ago but it's still destroying this family. Hank and Veronica are suffering. You girls are suffering. My mother is suffering, and it's because of me. If my dad were still around, every ounce of misery this family has experienced would never have happened. Saving Hank and Veronica and killing the Jabberwocky was the only way I knew to make things right. Maybe Mom would forgive me if I could make it right."

"She's your mother. She loves you."

Uncle Jake was quiet for a long time, then he stepped off the porch and started walking. "I just wanted to fix things," he said.

"Where are you going?" she asked, but he didn't answer.

• • •

The girls finished their lunch of BLTs with something that tasted like bacon but felt like pudding, and then had rose petal cookies for dessert. When their bellies were full, Granny collected the plates and took them into the kitchen. Daphne and Elvis ran upstairs to look after Puck. Sabrina went to the living room window and looked outside, hoping to find Uncle Jake making his way up the driveway. He wasn't there.

"Your mustache and goatee are starting to fade," Granny said when she returned to the dining room.

"I've been so busy I didn't even notice," Sabrina said, touching her lip lightly.

"Funny thing about time; it takes care of most problems," Granny said. "If you wait long enough, even a mountain becomes a valley." She pulled out a chair and invited Sabrina to sit down and join her.

"OK, bring it on," Sabrina said.

"What do you mean?"

"I know you're dying to give me a lecture on magic. I know you think its better not to use it."

"You think I hate magic?" Granny said.

"You don't?"

"No, I just believe it should be used as a last resort," she said. "Some people see it as the first solution to every problem and that leads to bigger problems."

"Well, a little magic could come in handy every time I'm running away from something that's trying to eat me."

Granny laughed. "You underestimate yourself, Sabrina. You don't need magic; you've got power coming out of your ears. You kept your sister safe for a year and a half in a very tough orphanage without magic. You escaped from one foster home after another without magic. You've been lost in the woods and chased by giants, you've foiled the destruction of this town, and saved all of our lives a couple times over and you did it all without magic. I know you think you're powerless, but you're wrong. You've got more power inside you than most full-grown adults ever will. You have a powerful heart, powerful friends, a powerful family, and a powerful mind. All of them have helped you overcome every obstacle that has gotten in your way, even when that obstacle happened to be two hundred feet tall or had a thousand teeth. Giving magic to you, child, would be a bit of overkill."

The old woman looked at the clock. "Well, Sabrina, do you think you could look after the house for about half an hour?"

"You're leaving me here alone with Daphne?" Sabrina said.

"Sure, you're eleven years old. I think you can be trusted for a little while," the old woman said. She took out a small whistle hanging from a chain around her neck and blew into it. Sabrina recognized it as the dog whistle the old woman used to call Mr. Canis.

"You do?" Sabrina cried. "Why?"

"Because I *want* to trust you," Granny replied as she rushed to get her handbag. "I hate to leave this work, but we can't ignore one crisis while we're working on another. I have to go down to the school and vote in the election. I'm afraid Mayor Charming is going to need every vote he can get."

She reached into her bag and took out the set of keys that unlocked everything in the house and in the Hall of Wonders and handed them to Sabrina.

Sabrina took the keys and looked down at them. It was an act of faith that no one had ever shown her before. A tear welled in her eye but she quickly wiped it away.

"But what about my addiction to magic?" Sabrina said.

"I've learned something from you, Sabrina. You can't run from your problems; you have to face them head-on. You'll never get over your need until you can walk away from it on your own."

"I have been nothing but a problem to you," Sabrina whispered.

The old woman hugged her. "If only everyone had the blessing of a problem like you."

The door opened and Mr. Canis entered. "Have you found a solution to the sword?"

"Not yet," Granny explained, "but democracy needs us, too. Have you given any more thought to voting for Charming?"

Mr. Canis growled.

Granny laughed and the two of them left. Seconds later, Sabrina heard the old family car's famous backfire and then they were gone.

Sabrina tucked the key ring into her pocket and looked down at the broken pieces of the sword laid out on the table.

"Spaulding, what are you trying to tell us?" Sabrina said.

Absentmindedly, she picked up the hilt of the Vorpal blade and aligned it with the broken pieces like she was working on some kind of incredibly sharp jigsaw puzzle. When all the pieces were aligned she closed her eyes and willed the sword to be whole.

Suddenly, the inscriptions on each piece glowed green. The letters flashed in bright red and then moved around of their own accord. A few of the letters jumped from the pieces of the blade they were on and landed on the piece that had no inscription. When this process was finished, the third piece of

the Vorpal blade had a clue of its own, one that glowed bright blue.

L F E H A U R B R A

"Spaulding, thank you!" Sabrina cried. "But, who is L . . . fehaur . . . bra!"

"What's going on?" Daphne said as she entered the room.

"Look!" Sabrina shouted. "The final clue appeared."

"I've never heard of anyone with that name," Daphne said.

"And I've never come across it in the journals," Sabrina said.

"Maybe it's not a name. Maybe it's a word puzzle," Daphne said.

Sabrina grabbed her sister and gave her a hug. "Daphne, you're brilliant!" The embrace gave Sabrina the same kind of charge she felt when she had held the Wand of Merlin.

"Of course I am," the little girl said.

"And we both know someone who likes word puzzles a lot," Sabrina said. "Come on!"

The two girls rushed up the steps and Sabrina unlocked the door that led to Mirror's room.

"You stole Granny's keys," Daphne cried.

"No she gave them to me. I'm babysitting you," Sabrina explained.

Daphne wrinkled up her nose. "That's crazy talk!"

Sabrina grabbed her hand and the two stepped inside the room. Sabrina braced for a bolt of lightning or a threatening ring of fire, but when Mirror's forbidding face appeared, two slices of cucumber were over his eyes.

"Who dares enter my domain!" he bellowed.

"Mirror! It's us!" Sabrina said.

Mirror reached up, removed a cucumber, and peered at the two girls. The clouds behind him quickly disappeared.

"Well, howdy, Grimm sisters," Mirror said. "Sorry about all the theatrics. I'm in the middle of my skin-care regimen. These cucumbers are lifesavers for my bags, but it's a two-hour ordeal every morning. Do yourself a favor, girls, and don't get old."

"We've collected all the pieces of the Vorpal blade," Daphne said.

"Impressive," Mirror replied.

"Each of the pieces had a clue on it to how to find the next," Sabrina explained. "Unfortunately, the last piece had no hints," she added. "Until we put the pieces together on the table. Then they glowed and some of the letters lit up like fireworks."

"We don't understand them but we thought you might," Daphne said.

Mirror looked surprised. "You want *my* help?"

"Well, I know you love word puzzles," Sabrina said.

Mirror grinned. "Wow! This is exciting. You know, most of the time I feel like I got stuck managing the supply closet while everyone else is out doing the exciting stuff. I don't think you Grimms have ever asked me for my help. Oh, I've been waiting for this for such a long time. Wait right there!"

Mirror's face disappeared from the reflection, but moments later he returned, wearing an old-fashioned hat and chomping on a pipe. He looked like a supernatural Sherlock Holmes.

"I'm sorry," Sabrina said. "We're in a bit of a hurry."

"Of course! What are the letters?"

"L-F-E-H-A-U-R-B-R-A," Sabrina said.

The letters suddenly appeared in the reflection. "What do you think it's supposed to tell you?" Mirror said.

"Who the Blue Fairy is," Daphne said.

Mirror's eyebrows rose in surprise. "Indeed! Well, let's have a look."

Suddenly the letters jumbled and were reformed into the words "Brael Rufha."

"I've got it!" Mirror said proudly "The Blue Fairy is actually Brael Rufha!"

"Who?" the girls asked.

Mirror studied the name. "Let's try that again."

The letters jumbled and collected themselves into a new name. "Harrab Fuel."

"I'm pretty sure there's no one in Ferryport Landing named Harrab Fuel," Sabrina said, trying to sound encouraging.

"I'm pretty sure no one in the world is named Harrab Fuel," Daphne added.

Mirror frowned at her and the letters swirled a final time. They rearranged into the word "blue," leaving the F, H, A, R, R, and A on the other side alone.

"All right, Blue Fharra," Mirror said. "Anyone know someone named Blue Fharra in this town?"

Sabrina jumped.

"You know, don't you?" Daphne said.

"Could you move the H to the end?" Sabrina said.

The letter floated over, making two new words: "Blue Farrah."

"The waitress!" Daphne continued. "Uncle Jake is not going to believe it. He's known her for years!"

"The Blue Fairy is a waitress?" Mirror said.

"Yes," Sabrina said. "At the Blue Plate Special. We met her yesterday. No wonder she was so relaxed when the Jabberwocky attacked. We've got to find her!"

"But how? Granny and Mr. Canis are gone and Uncle Jake took a hike," Daphne said.

Sabrina reached into her pocket and took out a business card—the card Rip van Winkle had handed her after he had driven the family to the school. "I know someone who can get us there."

"What about Puck? We can't leave him here alone," Daphne said.

"Mirror! You can look after him," Sabrina said, then turned to her sister. "Help me move Mirror into Granny's room."

The girls reached down and lifted with all their might, awkwardly carrying the enormous mirror out of the room.

"Girls! Be careful!" Mirror cried. "If you break me, it's going to take more than some cucumbers on the eyes to make me right."

• • •

When Rip van Winkle's cab pulled into the driveway, the girls ran out to it and jumped into the backseat. Elvis tumbled in as well and the girls shut the door.

"Take us to the Blue Plate Special," Sabrina shouted.

A snort and then a low snore was the driver's response. Rip van Winkle was asleep.

"You've got to be kidding me!" Sabrina shouted.

"Wake up!" Daphne yelled. "We have to go kill a monster."

Still there was nothing.

Each girl grabbed an ear and shouted as loudly as they could into it, but still Mr. van Winkle slumbered peacefully.

"We have to use the horn," Daphne said. "That's what woke him up the last time."

Sabrina leaped out of the car, opened the driver's door, and pushed down hard on the horn. There was a loud, gassy sound and a weak, fading honk followed by a clunk. Sabrina got down on her hands and knees. Underneath the car was a small, dangling mechanical device. She guessed it was the horn.

"It's broken!" she cried. "Everything on this car is broken!"

"What do we do? We have to get to the diner!"

Sabrina thought for a second and a crazy idea leaped into her head. She'd seen people drive cars. There were people in New York City who drove cabs who were nearly blind. How hard could it be?

"Get up in the front seat. I need your help," Sabrina said.

"You have a funny look on your face," Daphne said as she got out of the car.

"Help me push him over," Sabrina said. "We're driving."

"Nuh-uh! That's crazy talk!"

"It's the only choice we have," Sabrina said. "Don't worry. I've been watching how it works."

Elvis let out a whine from the backseat.

"Daphne, we have to do this!" she continued.

The little girl surrendered and together they pushed the old man to the passenger side of the cab.

"I need you to handle the pedals," Sabrina said. "My legs can't reach."

Daphne reluctantly crawled into the space beneath the dashboard.

"The one on the right is the gas and the other one is the brake," Sabrina explained.

"Crazy talk!" Daphne said, angrily.

Sabrina climbed into the driver's seat, adjusted the mirrors, and closed the door. She pulled the seatbelt over her shoulder and locked it into place. Then she took a deep breath and turned the key. The car roared to life.

"What do I do?" Daphne asked.

"Push on the gas," Sabrina said as she pulled the car's gearshift down into drive. The wheels squealed and the car lurched forward. *"Brake! Brake! Brake!"* she shouted but the car had already collided with the front porch. The mechanical Santa Claus crashed down from the roof onto the hood of the car. It's robotic "Ho! Ho! Ho!"s slowed and slurred until sparks shot out of Santa's ears and smoke billowed out from under his red cap.

"Aww, man. We are *so* getting coal for Christmas," Daphne said as she peeked over the dashboard at the mess.

"OK," Sabrina said, trying to relax. She looked down at the gearshift and realized she needed to put the taxi into reverse if she wanted to back out of the driveway. She pulled on the stick and the car rolled backward. When they reached the street, Sabrina turned the steering wheel and awkwardly guided the car onto the road. Then she put the car back into drive.

"Give it some gas," Sabrina said as they puttered along at five miles an hour.

"No!" Daphne said.

"It will take us a week to get there at this rate," Sabrina cried.

Daphne scowled and pushed hard on the gas. The car leaped forward and tore off down the road. Sabrina did her best to keep the old taxi on the pavement but it wasn't easy. The steering wheel had a significant pull to the right and the car kept veering into people's yards.

"There's a red light coming," Sabrina said.

Daphne pushed hard on the brake and the car stopped abruptly. Elvis rolled off the backseat and onto the floor.

This went on for several miles, with the girls passing only a few curious drivers who wisely steered their cars far away from the jalopy. It looked to Sabrina as if they were going to make it to the diner without too much damage, until they made a turn into Ferryport Landing's business district. She had always thought of the town as a slow, dull place. There was not a lot of traffic, but there were plenty of parked cars and with Sabrina's lack of experience, she slammed into several of them. Car alarms blasted, causing her to instinctively turn the car away from them only to find she was now in the oncoming traffic lane, scraping against the cars on the other side. The sound of screeching metal made her cringe.

Finally, they arrived at the Blue Plate Special and pulled into the parking lot of the diner. The girls hopped out and sprinted inside with Elvis in tow. The little bell rang roughly when they came through the door, causing a few customers to turn from their coffees and newspapers to see what all the commotion was about.

A heavyset waitress with tight brown curls and old-lady spectacles appeared with a handful of menus. When she saw Elvis she frowned. "Oh, girls, I'm sorry. We can't let you bring your . . . is that a dog?"

Sabrina ignored the question. "I'm looking for Farrah," she said as she and her sister scanned the restaurant. A horrible feeling crept over her as she eyed the place. Just two days ago this place had been a war zone. The Jabberwocky and Red Riding Hood had carved a path of destruction that only magic could have fixed in such a short time. Glinda the Good Witch and the rest of the Three often took care of such work for the mayor. It was their job to sprinkle forgetful dust on any non-Everafters traumatized by the unexpected appearance of monsters and the unexplained. *What if Farrah had gotten spooked and made sure she was forgotten as well?*

"Honey, she's not here," the waitress said.

Sabrina felt relieved. "Do you know where she is?"

"Why, she's on her lunch break," the waitress said with a slight bit of irritation.

Just then there was a loud thump that knocked a coffeepot to the floor. It shattered, sending coffee and glass everywhere.

"That sounds familiar," Daphne said, flashing her sister a worried look.

Sabrina grabbed the waitress by the shoulders. "Do you know where Farrah went?"

"Probably down to the elementary school. Today is election day," the woman replied.

The girls and the Great Dane raced outside and back into the cab.

"We have to go to the school," Sabrina cried.

Just then, a second loud thump actually lifted the taxi off the ground.

"Uh, we have a little problem," Daphne replied, pointing behind her.

The girls stared through the rear window. Standing behind the car was Red Riding Hood and her hulking nightmare, panting as if eagerly awaiting permission to rip them all limb from limb.

11

Sabrina nearly broke off the gearshift when she slammed it into drive. Daphne stomped hard on the gas until her foot was on the car's floorboard and the engine roared. The car lunged forward and raced across the parking lot; unfortunately, it didn't get far. The Jabberwocky leaped into the air and landed several yards in front.

"Brakes!" Sabrina shouted and Daphne obliged. The car slid to a stop inches from the monster's scaly leg.

Red Riding Hood skipped over to the car and tried to open the door, but Sabrina reached over just in time to lock it. The little girl scowled and pointed to the door. Her pet stepped over and tore it off its hinges.

"I know you are trying to ruin the game," Red Riding Hood said. "But I won't let you."

Sabrina slammed the car into reverse and out into the street. Then she put it in drive and made a hard right at the next intersection. When she checked her rearview mirror, the Jabberwocky was still behind them, with Red Riding Hood on its shoulders.

Sabrina made a hard left and then a quick right. Unfortunately, no matter how fast the cab went or how many turns she made, the monster and its mistress were gaining ground. They raced along the road that lined the Hudson River, and soon Sabrina saw the school. Red, white, and blue banners were everywhere, encouraging people to vote for mayor of Ferryport Landing. A small crowd of people stood outside in the parking lot and a few others shuffled out of the school's wide-open main doors.

"There it is!" Sabrina said. "Brake!"

Sabrina made a rough turn, hit a patch of ice, and sailed across the parking lot like a runaway train. "Brake again!" she cried.

Daphne pumped the brakes over and over but the old cab's bald tires had no traction and the car slid right through the main doors and down the hallway of the school. Voters screamed and leaped out of the way, narrowly escaping as the big car raced past them. The old jalopy crashed through the gymnasium's double doors and skidded to a stop.

A crowd gathered around the car as the girls climbed out. Many of them were outraged and demanding answers. Sabrina tried to warn them about the monsters chasing them, but no one would listen. Granny and Mr. Canis pushed through the mob and stood between it and the girls. The throngs of people quickly grew quiet. Sabrina wondered why and then noticed Mr. Canis staring everyone down. He sniffed the air wildly and then raised a curious eyebrow.

"Relda, the monster is coming. We have to get the humans to safety," he growled.

"A monster?" one woman cried. "Who is this lunatic?"

"He's right," Sabrina said. "We don't have time to explain to you, but he's not kidding. A real live monster is headed this way."

"Girls, what's going on?" Granny said.

"We know who the Blue Fairy is," Daphne said. She reached into the car and snatched the bag that contained the broken sword and handed it to her grandmother. "She's a waitress at the Blue Plate Special. Her name is Farrah."

"Relda, what is going on here?" Charming demanded.

"Later, Billy," Sabrina snapped. "We need to get these people out of here. There's a Jabberwocky coming."

"Mr. Seven, pull that fire alarm," the mayor commanded the little man. Mr. Seven rushed to the alarm and yanked it down hard. A siren wailed, drawing everyone's attention.

"There is a fire in the boiler room, people," Charming shouted. "Please evacuate to the parking lot."

"Thanks, Mayor," Granny Relda said. "Now we have to find Farrah."

"Who in the blazes is Farrah?" the mayor cried.

From the evacuating crowd stepped the waitress. She still had on her work uniform with its little nametag. She looked bewildered and vulnerable. "I am."

"I'm sorry to do this to you," Granny said, handing her the sack. "I know how important your privacy is, but we are in the middle of a dire emergency."

Farrah looked into the sack. "Of course," she said, removing the bubble gum from her mouth. Granny quickly tore a sheet of paper out of the notebook she kept in her purse and handed it to the woman, who used it to wrap up the sticky substance.

Suddenly, a sky-blue light began to seep out of Farrah's clothing. It engulfed her body and grew so bright it made her impossible to look at. When the light dimmed, Farrah the waitress was gone. In her place was a tall, beautiful woman with light blue hair and skin like milk. Her eyes were twinkling stars and she had two pink-streaked wings on her back that fluttered softly.

"It's the Blue Fairy," someone said from the crowd. Many

of the Everafters who had exited the gymnasium rushed back in to get a good look at the mysterious figure.

The Blue Fairy held out her hand and a little ball of blue light appeared. It crackled with electricity and Sabrina could hear a soft humming sound coming from it. The ball zipped out of her hand and flew into the sack that held the sword pieces. The bag immediately filled with blue light. After a moment, the light faded and the Blue Fairy reached inside. When she removed her hand, she was holding the Vorpal blade, perfect and whole.

Granny took it eagerly from the woman and thanked her.

"Relda, give me the sword," Mr. Canis said. "You can't handle the monster and the child."

"You are in no condition, old friend. Don't worry; I've had to fight a lot of monsters in my day. I suspect there will be plenty more," she said and then turned to the crowd. "Folks, I recommend that you find somewhere safe to hide. Something wicked this way comes."

As if on cue, the Jabberwocky, with Red Riding Hood on its shoulders, stepped into the room. The monster set the little girl on the ground and sized up the crowd as if deciding whom to eat and in what order.

"Grandma! Doggy!" Red Riding Hood cried as she rushed

toward Granny Relda and Mr. Canis. "I have my family back. Now we can play house."

Granny lifted the sword threateningly.

"My, what a big sword you have, Grandma," Red Riding Hood continued.

"Child, I am not your grandmother," Granny said. "The two people you have kidnapped are not your mother and father. Your family is dead. They died hundreds of years ago and nothing you can do will bring them back. Pretending to have a family is not the same as having one."

"But we can play house," the little girl said.

"Playtime is over, little one. Where are Henry and Veronica Grimm?"

Sabrina thought she saw a glimmer of understanding in the little girl's face. As she stared up at Granny Relda, Red Riding Hood seemed to have a million terrible questions to ask. Maybe it was all too overwhelming for her, because she shook her head violently and her contorted, insane expression returned.

"Kitty! Let's take Grandmother and Doggy home with us," she shouted.

Granny raised the Vorpal blade to defend herself, but the monster was on top of her in a flash. It grabbed her around the waist and lifted her off the ground. The old woman dropped the sword and it clanged loudly on the gymnasium floor.

"Granny!" the girls shouted.

Mr. Canis leaped at the beast but a flick of its tail sent the old man sailing across the room and into the crowd.

"I'll go for the sword," Sabrina said. She dashed across the floor, but before she could reach it, the monster slammed its foot down on top of it. Sabrina tried to pull it out from under the beast but it was too heavy.

Just then, Sheriff Hamstead rushed through the crowd. He had his billy club held high. "Put her down!" he shouted. The monster turned toward the pudgy policeman and swatted the cop across the gym with one of its awesome paws. Hamstead sailed through the crowd and landed painfully at the foot of the podium. Snow White tried to rush to his side but Charming grabbed her arm and held her back.

"I have to help them," Snow White cried.

"You'll get yourself killed," he said. "There's nothing anyone in this room can do to stop that thing."

"Billy, what happened to you?" Snow White said. "Where's my white knight?"

Sabrina tugged at the sword once more, but still couldn't free it. When the monster turned all of his attention on her,

Daphne took advantage of its distraction. Sabrina watched helplessly as her sister rushed to the monster's side.

"First you bow to your opponent," Daphne said and then bowed to the monster who was now hovering over her.

"Daphne, no!" Sabrina cried.

"Don't worry," Daphne cried. "Ms. White taught us that these moves will stop an attacker much bigger than yourself.

"Move into offensive stance," Daphne continued, shifting her body into her attack stance with fists clenched. "Present your warrior face! Argggghhhh!"

The beast looked down at her and roared so loudly that Daphne's hair flew back.

Unfazed by the monster's scream, Daphne rushed forward. "Deliver attack!" She kicked the Jabberwocky in the leg, but her assault was like a mosquito biting an elephant. The beast reached down and picked the little girl off the floor with its free hand. Now it had both Sabrina's grandmother and her sister in its deadly grasp.

Sabrina looked to the crowd of Everafters for help. Ms. White looked as if she wanted to but was held fast by Charming. Mr. Canis and Sheriff Hamstead were still recovering from the Jabberwocky's attack. Most everyone else was cowering in fear. There were no heroes to save them. Sabrina caught a glimpse of the Queen of Hearts. She stood off to the side with a wicked smile.

Suddenly, there was a *pop*! Uncle Jake appeared out of thin air high above the Jabberwocky. He landed on top of the monster's back and wrapped his arms around its neck. Moments later, unable to hold the beast, he was flung to the floor. But the man's sudden appearance had surprised the beast, and it dropped Granny Relda and Daphne.

"Sorry to keep you waiting, ladies," Uncle Jake said, helping his mother and the little girl to their feet. He tapped the Nome King's belt wrapped around his waist and shrugged. "Do you know how hard it is to find thirty size-D batteries?"

The monster roared in frustration and took a step toward the family. It was all Sabrina needed. She snatched the blade off the ground and held it over her head. One swift slice would bring her family home. It would save Puck and get him to safety. Suddenly, there was a hand on her shoulder. She turned and found Uncle Jake.

" 'Brina, this belongs to me," he said as he took the sword away from her. Sabrina looked into his face and saw a broken heart finally getting its revenge. This monster had killed Uncle Jake's father. It had decimated his family, forcing his mother to erase his existence. It had helped kidnap his brother and sister-in-law. It had brought misery on the girls. Sabrina stepped aside. Uncle Jake walked calmly over to the Jabberwocky as if he had been preparing for this moment all his life. He glanced over at Red Riding Hood as if to say, "It's over," and then plunged the sword deep into the beast's belly.

The Jabberwocky's death cry was oddly faint and pathetic. Uncle Jake pulled the sword out again, aimed it where the monster's heart might have been, and sank it deep into its flesh. There was a moment of calmness on the beast's face and then it fell over as if it had been pushed. When it tumbled to the ground it caused the gymnasium's shiny hardwood floor to buckle. The monster's little leathery wings flapped for a few moments and then grew still.

"You killed the kitty!" Red Riding Hood raged. "You ruined the game!"

Daphne stepped over to the girl, bowed, presented her warrior face, and then punched Red Riding Hood in the face. She fell over unconscious.

"Crazy talk," Daphne said to the crumpled girl.

Uncle Jake yanked the blade from the monster and held it in his hands. He looked as if he wanted to kill the monster all over again.

"It's over, Jake," Granny said.

"Is it?" he said, as several Everafters approached: Snow White, Sheriff Hamstead, the Queen of Hearts, Sheriff Nottingham, as well as a collection of talking animals, Munchkinlanders, and trolls. The Blue Fairy was at their center.

"This is an outrage!" the Queen of Hearts screamed. "This was a deliberate action by Mayor Charming and his cronies, the family Grimm, to disrupt this election. I wouldn't be surprised if this was an attempt to sway voters into believing this family has value in this community. Well, it won't work!"

"If you don't shut your mouth right now, I'm going to shut it for you," Snow White said.

"You insolent cow," Nottingham said. "You may be the mayor's trollop, but your demands mean little to me." He pulled his sword from his waist and stalked toward the Grimms. "Even if we don't win this election, things are going to change right now."

Suddenly, an arrow zipped through the air and impaled Nottingham's hand. His sword fell to the ground and he cried out in agony.

"You won't lay a hand on the Grimms as long as I live," a voice bellowed. Sabrina turned and nearly fell over in shock. Mayor Charming stood on the stage, bow in hand and with another arrow set to fly. A man in a green suit stood next to him. He had bright red hair and a bushy goatee.

"I told you he was in league with them," the queen cried.

"Think what you want," Charming said. "But they're going home today, safe and sound. Right after they vote for me, of course. And Nottingham, the next time you call the woman I love a trollop, you'll find an arrow in your throat."

Nottingham scowled and stormed out of the room. Charming handed the bow and arrow to the man in the green suit. "Thank you, Robin," he said.

"He saved us," Sabrina said.

"Ending his career in the process, I fear," Granny Relda replied. "Look at the crowd. He just lost this election."

"Why would he do that?"

Granny pointed at the mayor. He and Snow White were kissing passionately as if they were the only two people on the planet.

"Love can make a hero out of anyone," Granny replied.

"I knew he was one of the good guys," Daphne said.

"Well, people, don't let this obvious attempt to disrupt the election stop you from casting your ballots," the queen said. "This is exactly the kind of nonsense that needs to change in Ferryport Landing."

"You want a change?" Uncle Jake shouted. "I'll give you a change!" He spun around, grabbed the Blue Fairy around the neck, and held the Vorpal blade to her throat.

"Jake, what are you doing?" Granny cried.

"There's more to fix!" Uncle Jake shouted. "And the Blue Fairy is going to help me."

"What do you want?" the Blue Fairy asked softly.

"Is it true that if I wish for something you have to fulfill it?"

The radiant fairy nodded.

"Then I want a wish," Uncle Jake said.

"Uncle Jake!" Sabrina cried. "What are you thinking? She helped us."

"She's going to help us a lot more! What's it going to be, Blue?" Jake demanded.

The Blue Fairy looked Jake in the eye. "I hope your wish gives you what you need. You have your wish."

"I wish I had all of your power!" Uncle Jake said.

The Blue Fairy smiled and nodded as if what he was asking for was simple. A swirl of light and mist encircled her, then turned into a pulsating orb as big as a baseball. It flew at Uncle Jake, hitting him hard in the chest, and then there was a tremendous explosion that knocked everyone off their feet. When Sabrina stood up again, she saw the Blue Fairy lying on the floor nearby. Her magic was gone and she had changed back into Farrah the waitress.

"Hey, 'Brina," Uncle Jake said behind her. She spun around

to face him. Two pink-streaked wings suddenly popped out of his back. He turned his head to look at them. They flapped and lifted him off the ground, allowing him to hover above the crowd. He laughed like a child on Christmas morning.

"Can you believe this?" he said overjoyed.

Sabrina looked to her grandmother. Granny Relda was full of despair. "Jake, what have you done?"

"It's not what I've done, Mom," he said as he floated back down to the ground and kissed her on the cheek. "It's what I'm going to do! You wouldn't believe the power! It's like a waterfall, like the sun. I'm bigger than life, bigger than even the most powerful Everafter. I'm the kind of thing they write stories about!"

He looked out over the crowd of Everafters and his face grew serious. "But I need more."

He raised his hands and a bright blue ball appeared in them. The ball shot electrical charges through the crowd, hitting every Everafter squarely in the chest. Mr. Canis fell to his knees. Snow White collapsed on Charming, who fell himself. The White Rabbit tumbled to the ground and was squished by Beauty and her beastly husband. Ogres, cyclopses, trolls, witches, and even fairy godmothers collapsed under their own weight.

"What are you doing to them?" Sabrina begged.

"I'm taking the magic that makes them immortal. I need it," he shouted as the energy surged through him. His eyes disappeared and were replaced with a fiery light. Cracks appeared all over his body as if it were just a useless shell and then a light flashed through the gymnasium so brightly Sabrina had to close her eyes. Uncle Jake rocketed off the ground, through the roof, and into the sky. Rubble and debris fell from ceiling. Sabrina grabbed her grandmother and sister and pulled them to safety.

"What's he doing?" Daphne asked, but Granny didn't answer. She stared at the hole in the roof. Sabrina had her eyes elsewhere. The Everafters lying scattered around the gym were growing older at an alarming rate. Prince Charming's youthful, handsome face began to sag. His eyes took on a slightly yellow tint and his hair started falling out. He was becoming an old man right before her eyes. He reached out for her with a bony, frail hand.

Mr. Canis morphed into the Wolf but the beast wasn't his intimidating, deadly self. He struggled with age as his dark brown coat turned white and his eyes grew cloudy with blindness.

"Look!" Daphne said as she pointed to the ceiling. Uncle Jake was back.

He descended like an angel enveloped in a light so bright the girls had to look away. When he landed on the ground, he smiled at his family and the light faded. The Uncle Jake that Sabrina knew was gone, replaced with someone completely new who seemed to be made of diamonds. The only thing left, she noticed, was his quirky, mischievous grin. He stepped forward to hug the two sisters but they stepped back in fear.

"What have you done?" Sabrina asked.

"I'm granting myself a wish," he replied. "I wanted to be powerful enough to make the people I love happy. I've been miserable, Sabrina. Happy is better. You can be happy, too. Wish for something, Sabrina. Anything. I can make it happen."

"But look at the cost!" Granny Relda said as she hovered over Mayor Charming's elderly body. Snow White lay next to him, reaching for his hand with her bony, arthritic fingers. "The price is too high."

"Don't cry for them," Uncle Jake said. "The Everafters have had their day in the sun and it was a long, long day. With their power, I can re-create this world as a paradise where 'happily ever after' isn't just for a bunch of bedtime stories come to life. It's time for all of our dreams to come true! And I'm starting with you."

Suddenly, the pulsating blue orb reappeared in his hand. It twisted and turned until it divided itself in two, creating an identical twin. He tossed the second orb to the ground at Granny Relda's feet and once it was at rest it grew in size, morphing and bending. When the transformation was complete, an old man stood in its place. He had broad shoulders, blond-streaked gray hair, a beard, and a familiar toothy smile. Sabrina had seen him many times in photographs hanging throughout the house, but that was the only place the old man still existed. He was Basil Grimm, the girls' grandfather and Granny Relda's husband.

"Relda?" the old man asked, looking slightly confused.

Granny Relda burst into tears and buried her face in her hands. The old man rushed to her side and embraced her, but she pulled away.

"It's not right," the old woman said. "Send him back."

"No!" Uncle Jake cried. Discouraged, he turned to Daphne and smiled. "I know something you want." The blue orb divided again and the man tossed its duplicate at the little girl's feet. Once again, the orb grew and morphed, but this time, instead of creating another person, it became a door, standing in space, and someone was knocking on the other side.

"Open it," the man said. "It's for you."

Daphne backed away from the door and shook her head. Uncle Jake frowned but then raised his hand and the door swung open on its own. Behind the door were Henry and Veronica Grimm. They rushed through the doorway and swept the little girl up in their arms, kissing her over and over dozens of times. Henry and Veronica raced to Sabrina and embraced her as well.

"It's like a dream," Sabrina said.

"Okay 'Brina, what'll it be?" Uncle Jake said. "Make a wish. But I already know what you want. You want power, and not like that crummy wand you had to surrender. I'm talking real power—the kind that moves mountains and boils rivers. Your family would never die. You would always be happy. No more monsters. No more fairy tales. You could change everything."

Sabrina's heart raced with possibilities. Just standing near Uncle Jake was like an incredible feeling, more intense than holding the Wand of Merlin, more like *being* the wand itself. With the kind of power Uncle Jake offered she could erase the last year and a half like they had never happened; no orphanage, no giants, no monsters, no bad guys. She could heal Puck. There were no limits to the possibilities. Her imagination washed over her, showing her millions of options for a happy life.

"Sabrina," Granny said. "How much are you willing to pay?"

Sabrina glanced around the room at the Everafters. Some of them had already died. Others were pulling in their final breaths. Was her happiness worth their lives? Worse, could she resist the temptation even if she knew what the right thing to do was?

"I know what I want, Uncle Jake," Sabrina said.

Uncle Jake smiled and gave her a wink. "Make it count!"

"Uncle Jake, you're smart, you've got a great family, and you're a Grimm," Sabrina said. "I wish that deep down you had always known how much power that gave you."

Uncle Jake looked strange. His eyes began to well with tears and then the school began to rumble. Suddenly, a flood of memories rolled through Sabrina's mind. She watched how she had met her Uncle Jake and how he taught her to use the wand. She watched Granny Relda catch them in the Hall of Wonders, and their battle with the Jabberwocky at the diner. She even saw some of her nightmares flash in front of her, as well as the dramatic return of Mr. Canis. It all happened the same way it had, except for one shocking difference. When Uncle Jake killed the Jabberwocky, the fight was over. He didn't attack the Blue Fairy. He was content with how it ended and he hugged his mother.

Sabrina opened her eyes. Her grandfather was gone and so were her parents. The Everafters were alive and well and gathered around her. The Queen of Hearts was still filling the air with her angry tirade and the Jabberwocky was still dead at their feet. The Blue Fairy stood next to her, smiling. "Thank you, Sabrina," she said, and then she transformed into a glowing orb and zipped away.

Uncle Jake stepped over to Red Riding Hood and snatched the magical ring off the little girl's finger and tucked it into his pants pocket. Granny frowned but Uncle Jake just laughed. "Don't worry, Mom. It's going straight into the Hall of Wonders for safekeeping."

"Hello, Grandmother," Red Riding Hood said, waking up and climbing to her feet. "My kitty is dead."

"Child, I am not your . . ."

"Play along," Sabrina suggested.

Granny looked unsure, but nodded. "We don't need the kitty to play games. We can play without him."

Red Riding Hood looked to the ceiling as if debating what the old woman was saying. A smile crossed her face and she clapped her hands. "Okie-dokie!"

"But before we play games, we need our whole family together, right?"

The little girl nodded.

"So we need to find the mommy and the daddy and the baby brother and then we'll all go and get the puppy and then we can play house. Does that sound good?"

"Yes, I want to play house," the child repeated. "But, the master will be mad if I tell."

"The master?" Sabrina cried.

"Yes, he would be very mad. He wants to keep the mommy and daddy and the baby brother. He wants me to paint the red hands everywhere I go. I try to be good. The master can get angry."

"She's not the leader of the Scarlet Hand," Daphne said.

"Well, I don't think the master would mind if we all played, would he?" Granny continued.

"I guess not," the little girl said.

• • •

Sheriff Hamstead had Henry and Veronica's sleeping bodies transported to Granny's house in an ambulance. Now they both rested on a queen-sized bed inside the room that also housed the magic mirror.

"Are they sick?" Daphne asked as she held her mother's hand.

"No, *liebling*. Just sleeping," Granny Relda said.

Sabrina put her head on her father's chest and heard his heart beating. Then she reached up and kissed him on the forehead. "Did they find the baby?" she asked.

"No sign of it," Sheriff Hamstead said. "All that was there was an empty bassinet."

"Why won't they wake up?" Daphne asked.

"It's a sleeping spell," Granny explained.

"And a strong one at that," Mirror said as his face appeared in the reflection. "I'm sure we don't have anything in the Hall of Wonders that can break it."

"Then what can we do?" Sabrina said.

"These sleeping spells . . . some of them are fairly normal potions, sometimes poisoned flowers or apples, but overwhelmingly they are cast by someone with a vendetta against the victim," Uncle Jake said. "Luckily, even bad magic has a backup plan, and in nearly every case I've ever heard, the spell can be broken with a kiss."

Elvis hopped up on his back paws and licked Veronica on the face.

"Elvis, this is my mom," Daphne explained to the big dog. "You're going to love her."

"I kissed Dad on the forehead. Why didn't he wake up?" said Sabrina

"It has to be a romantic kiss from someone who truly loves them," Granny Relda explained.

"If one of them was awake then this would be no problem," Mr. Canis said.

"Wait, if that's how you break the spell, how are we going to wake them?" Sabrina said. "My parents love each other. They are the only ones that could wake each other up."

When no one answered, Sabrina thought she might cry.

"We'll find a way," Granny said as she took Sabrina into her arms.

"In the meantime, we should address the problem with Puck," Mr. Canis said. "He is growing weaker. If we can use the Vorpal blade to cut a big enough hole in the barrier, I'd like to take the car and get the boy to his people."

"I'll go with you," Hamstead said. "I happen to be between jobs at the moment."

"The Queen of Hearts won the election?" Daphne cried.

"By a landslide," Hamstead grumbled.

"Oh, dear," Granny said.

Sabrina stared down at her parents. She knew they would understand. "I'll go, too. Puck would never have been hurt if he weren't trying to help us find Mom and Dad. I owe it to him."

"Me, too!" Daphne said.

"Jacob, can I trust you in the house all alone?" Granny asked her son.

Uncle Jake smiled. "Probably not, but I'll keep the place safe."

• • •

Mr. Canis helped Granny Relda put Puck in the front seat of the car and then helped her in as well. When everyone had

squeezed into the jalopy, Uncle Jake waved and wished them them all the luck in the world.

"You be careful among the Faerie folk," Uncle Jake said. "If you think this town is full of nuts, you haven't seen anything yet."

"We'll be careful," Sabrina said.

"Take care of my Elvis," Daphne said. The big dog leaped up to her window and gave her a farewell lick on the face.

Mr. Canis started the car and backed it out of the driveway.

"We're an odd group of people for an adventure, don't you think?" Hamstead squealed.

Granny smiled. "Pig and Wolf and Grandma. Who would have thought it?"

Even Mr. Canis laughed. Sabrina hoped he would never do it again. It was an obnoxious snorty sound.

Daphne hugged her sister. "This isn't exactly how I pictured our first Christmas in Ferryport Landing."

Sabrina gazed out the window as the car rolled down the road. Would they be able to save Puck? Would they find a way to wake their parents? And would the family Grimm ever get its happily ever after?

To be continued in

THE SISTERS GRIMM

BOOK FOUR

ONCE UPON A CRIME

ABOUT THE AUTHOR

Michael Buckley is the *New York Times* best-selling author of the Sisters Grimm series. He has also written and developed television shows for many networks. *The Mole People* and *The New Sideshow* can be seen regularly on the Discovery Channel. Michael lives in New York City.

This book was designed by Jay Colvin and art directed by Becky Terhune. It is set in Adobe Garamond, a typeface that is based on those created in the sixteenth century by Claude Garamond. Garamond modeled his typefaces on those created by Venetian printers at the end of the fifteenth century. The modern version used in this book was designed by Robert Slimbach, who studied Garamond's historic typefaces at the Plantin-Moretus Museum in Antwerp, Belgium.

The capital letters at the beginning of each chapter are set in Daylilies, designed by Judith Sutcliffe. She created the typeface by decorating Goudy Old Style capitals with lilies.